THE Downtown Desperadoes

Children's Books by
Sigmund Brouwer

FROM BETHANY HOUSE PUBLISHERS

www.coolreading.com

05A

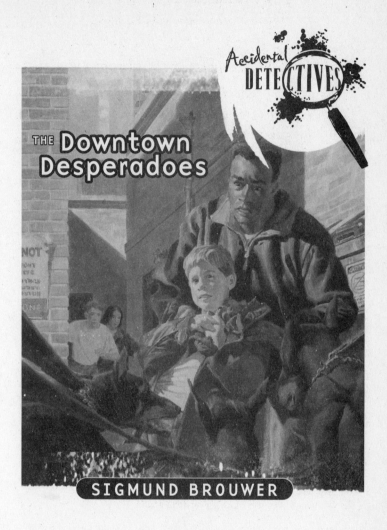

THE **Downtown Desperadoes**

Accidental DETECTIVES

SIGMUND BROUWER

BETHANY HOUSE
MINNEAPOLIS, MINNESOTA

Published by Bethany House Publishers
11400 Hampshire Avenue South
Bloomington, Minnesota 55438
www.bethanyhouse.com

Bethany House Publishers is a division of
Baker Publishing Group, Grand Rapids, Michigan.

Printed in the United States of America

Library of Congress Cataloging-in-Publication Data

Brouwer, Sigmund, 1959–
    The downtown desperadoes / by Sigmund Brouwer
      p.   cm. — (Accidental detectives)
    Summary: When Ricky and his friends and family forego a planned vacation to return to New York City to help an old friend, they become involved in a mystery which includes blackmail, arson, and lost love.
    ISBN 0-7642-2576-6 (pbk.)
    [1. Mistaken identity—Fiction. 2. New York (N.Y.)—Fiction. 3. Christian life—Fiction. 4. Mystery and detective stories.] I. Title.
    PZ7.B79984Do 2004
    [Fic]—dc22   2004012763

SIGMUND BROUWER is the award-winning author of scores of books. He speaks to kids around the continent in an effort to instill good reading and writing habits in the next generation. Sigmund and his wife, Cindy Morgan, divide their time between Tennessee and Alberta, Canada.

For Olivia
and the sunshine you bring
into this world

CHAPTER 1

You know you're in trouble when the seventy-eight-year-old woman in your mom's kitchen tells you it's the first meal she has cooked in twenty-five years.

"Oh, it probably sounds silly," Miss Bugsby giggled as she set dishes in front of us on the table, "but I'm absolutely thrilled to have this chance. For all that time, my only company was the servants. And *they* did all the cooking for *me*."

She pranced back to the stove and lifted the lid from a pot. A cloud swirled around her head, so that it was difficult to tell her gray hair from the rising vapors.

Mike Andrews elbowed my ribs. "I want to make it to my next birthday," he hissed into my ear.

"Ralphy and me, too," I whispered back. "We're too young to be poisoned to death."

"Did you say something, Ricky?" Miss Bugsby called from the vapors. Cheerfulness and joy rang from her voice.

Which was a switch.

Barely a few months earlier Ralphy Zee, who sat across from me, and Mike and I had thought Miss Bugsby was the meanest woman in our small town of Jamesville. Then a decades-old mystery about her father—one I thought of as the *Race for the Park Street Treasure*—had been solved, and she was a different person.

Now the only thing the same about her was the head-to-toe black dresses she still wore. And even that was changing. Tonight her shoes were red, which, as Ralphy had mentioned, was quite bold for a lady her age.

"I'm *so* glad your parents trusted me to come over to your house while they went out," Miss Bugsby continued without waiting for my answer. Mom and Dad had taken my little sister, Rachel, with them to some parenting group thing that I didn't want to know anything about. "And I'm *so* glad that Mike and Ralphy could visit. None of you realize how much it means to cook for hungry boys. I *do* hope you like it."

"I'm sure we will," Ralphy said bravely.

"I'm so glad to hear that," she said as she brought her first pot to the table. "I was worried that you might not like cabbage soup."

She hummed as she ladled it into our bowls.

Joel, my six-year-old brother, began slurping it before she could fill the rest of our bowls.

Wonderful, I thought, *the little traitor's going to make the rest of us look bad.*

"Joel," I said. "Pray first."

He scowled at me but stopped eating until Miss Bugsby had returned to the table and said grace. Then he slurped with a vengeance.

Miss Bugsby's smile spread widely across the wrinkles of her high cheekbones. "I'm so relieved," she said. "I've worried about this all week."

A timer on the stove began clanging, and she hopped from her chair back to the remaining pots and pans.

I took my first tiny taste of the purple broth.

"How is it, boys?" she called without looking back. "There's more, you know."

It was, well, cabbage soup.

By the looks on Ralphy's and Mike's faces, I could tell they thought the same. My only consolation was something I had planned for Mike during the main course.

Mike Andrews was the kind of guy always in mismatched high-top sneakers and a gaudy Hawaiian shirt that made your eyes hurt. Red hair. Freckles. A perpetual New York Yankees baseball cap, and a grin as wide as a Halloween pumpkin. He was born to try anything that looked impossible, and he lived to play jokes on friends.

Right then I owed him one.

Barely a week earlier he had convinced me that Ralphy's birthday party was a costume party because it was so close to Halloween. Unfortunately, I had believed him. There is nothing funny—no matter what Mike says—about wearing a clown outfit for two hours while everyone else is in jeans and sweatshirts.

My revenge for that was in a tiny bottle in my back pocket, filled with hot, hot Tabasco sauce.

"Eat all your soup," I whispered to Mike. "It'll break her heart if you don't."

He nodded sorrowful agreement at me and choked back spoonful after spoonful. Ralphy and I did the same.

"Now for the main course," Miss Bugsby announced. "A recipe handed down from my grandmother to my mother. A closely guarded family secret. It's a Scottish version of onion, carrot, and lamb stew."

She brought it back to the table. By the look of hopeful fear on her face, I knew that no matter how terrible it tasted, I would eat every bite and pretend it tasted great.

It meant, of course, that Mike, too, would force himself to get through that meal for the same reason.

"Did you say something?" I asked Mike as I quickly turned to him with the last spoonful of cabbage soup almost to my mouth. "Ooooops. I'm sorry, Mike."

Imagine that, I commented to myself, *spilling on his shirt.* "There's a towel in the bathroom, pal," I told him. "That soup should wipe clean in a flash."

"Brilliant move, Einstein," he mumbled as he pushed away from the table.

"Hurry back," Miss Bugsby said, "or your stew will get cold."

I nearly giggled. *No, it won't,* I thought.

Mike trudged to the bathroom, and Miss Bugsby turned back to the stove.

"Who's at the window, Ralphy?" I whispered as I reached into my pocket for the bottle.

He may be a computer genius, but sometimes Ralphy's not too bright. He squirmed in his chair to see, and in the few seconds while Joel and I had the table to ourselves, I splashed Mike's stew with at least a quarter of the bottle.

Hah! See if Mike Andrews ever sends me to a party in a clown outfit again.

"I don't see anybody," Ralphy said.

Before I could answer, the phone rang. "Will you get that, Ricky?" Miss Bugsby asked from beside the stove. "I don't want this pudding to burn."

I reached the phone before the third ring. As I answered, Mike passed me on his way back from the bathroom and merely scowled.

"Hello. This is the Kidd residence."

"I . . . need . . . your . . . help."

"I beg your pardon, sir?"

Brief silence. Then, "Find . . . me . . . at . . . the . . . end . . . of . . . circle. . . ." A long pause. The voice was hoarse. "Remember . . . subway."

"Is this a prank call?" I asked.

A muffled shout somewhere in the background came through the telephone.

The voice groaned, then said in a new tone with forced effort for loudness, "Medium pizza, please. Extra cheese, anchovy fish, ham. Don't forget the anchovy fish and—"

Click.

The dial tone buzzed in my ear.

I returned to the table and shrugged as they looked at me. "I have no idea. Some weirdo."

I sat down and took a deep breath. The ordeal of stew was in front of me, and Miss Bugsby hovered nearby with anxious glances in my direction.

To buy time, I fumbled with my napkin and glanced over at Mike.

His eyes were watering already. *Got him!*

"Good stew?" I asked him with as much innocence as I could manage.

"I never knew it could taste like this," he choked.

I smiled at Miss Bugsby.

"I think that means Mike loves it, ma'am." I smiled again. "Perhaps he'll tell you about Ralphy's birthday party."

I elbowed Mike as I continued to speak to her. "He's got a great story about playing a joke on someone."

Miss Bugsby smiled back. "I want to hear all about it. Just let me finish with this pudding."

She turned back to the stove and resumed stirring the last pot on the stovetop.

I elbowed Mike again and whispered from the side of my mouth, "How's *my* joke on *you* taste?"

He gulped water from his nearly empty glass. "The first three swallows are killing me."

I smothered laughter. *Revenge is so sweet.*

Ralphy pointed behind me. "Why'd you leave the phone off the hook?"

"Huh?"

I followed his finger with my eyes.

"It's not off the—"

How could I have fallen for that old line? By the time I realized what was happening, it was too late. In the short time it took to look away from the table, Mike had finished switching plates with me.

And Miss Bugsby was already halfway back to the table.

She sat down and smoothed a napkin across her lap. She searched my face with expectant eyes.

"How is it, Ricky?"

Ralphy smiled.

Mike smiled.

They both waited like smug foxes in a henhouse.

"The stew, ma'am?" I asked.

"Yes. The closely guarded family secret. How is it?"

"Just, um . . . taking my first bite now."

I put a spoonful in my mouth and gulped it down. It felt like someone had opened my jaws wide and fired a blowtorch down my throat.

"Gaaaakkk!" I coughed. "I mean, great!"

I coughed again. "It certainly is unlike any meal I've had before."

"I'm going to have a second helping," Mike said to me. "So you'd better eat quickly. Otherwise there will be none left for you."

Miss Bugsby beamed. "Yes, Ricky, don't be shy. Go ahead. It's such a compliment when a boy eats every bite."

Flames continued down into my stomach and started a bonfire that scorched its way back up and out my nose.

I nodded, then forced another spoonful into my mouth.

I blinked back a tear of anguish. "Ma'am," I asked, "any chance I could have a little more water?"

CHAPTER 2

Tabasco sauce is a great way to encourage someone to brush his teeth. But three times did not help in the slightest. Each little burp—and Tabasco sauce fills you with too many little burps—shot fire through my throat and mouth long after Miss Bugsby and Mike and Ralphy had gone home.

In the middle of frantic toothbrushing number four, Mom interrupted by tapping on the bathroom door.

"You should have been in your bedroom fifteen minutes ago."

I opened the door without pulling the toothbrush from my mouth.

"Aaah gaw brug maa teee!" *I've got to brush my teeth!*

She shook her head. "It doesn't take half an hour. Your brother needs in."

I nodded, then wiped toothpaste drool from my chin.

As I pushed the door closed with my foot, a word echoed through my mind.

Brother. Brother. Brother.

Slowly and thoughtfully, I pushed my toothbrush back and forth.

Brother. Brother. Why did that bother me so much?

It wasn't the mention of Joel that filled me with vague unease. No, *that* brother terrified me twenty-six hours a day. He's a tiny ghost, coming and going like smoke on a windy day, and he spends most of his time following my friends and me around Jamesville.

He never says much when you do spot him . . . which isn't often. He just stares and watches the heart attack he just gave you by appearing from nowhere. Then disappears again when you blink your eyes. Worse, he always manages to do it during the times you want to be alone the most. It's like having a second conscience whenever yours fails.

Without his teddy bear, he'd be invincible. I use it as hostage or bait, depending on the situation. One of my best moves is to hang it from a branch in our backyard. Joel will sit beneath the teddy bear for hours and gaze patiently upward until someone finally rescues it, giving me, of course, those same hours without the fear of being followed.

No, I told myself as I chewed on my toothbrush, Joel wasn't the reason that word echoed inside like untuned guitar strings.

Brother. Brother.

Then an image hit me.

Just before summer vacation, our entire class had visited New York. It would have been the perfect school trip, except for one complication. Joel. Within a day, he had disappeared completely.

Mike, Ralphy, and our friend Lisa Higgins were sick with worry about it, enough to slip away from the hotel with me at night and begin our own search.

I barely felt the toothbrush in my hand as I remembered the image.

Because, crazy as it sounds, that search had taken Mike and me to a run-down café in downtown Manhattan, long after midnight. A gruff man behind the counter there—Hugo—warned us about the terrors that Joel faced as a street person, someone without a home in the concrete loneliness of New York City. Mike and I had started to sink even lower into depression when the door to the diner opened.

As I remembered, the image grew stronger, and all I had to do to bring back our time in the New York diner was close my eyes. . . .

Hugo's face split into a wide grin as he looked toward the door. "Hey, Brother Phillip! Good to see you! The usual?"

"You bet, Hugo." The voice behind our shoulders was deep and soft. I peeked back, expecting to see someone handsome and tall and well-dressed.

Wrong. At least about the well-dressed part. His pants were made of a rough brown material, and his shirt was frayed at the collar and cuffs of the sleeves. He might have been handsome, except his hair was shaggy and his face was pale and tired under a few days' growth of beard. One of the street people?

Brother Phillip sat on a nearby stool. He nodded at Mike and me.

"Good evening, gentlemen," he said in that comforting voice. "How are you tonight?" He leaned over Mike and gravely shook the teddy bear's paw as if two twelve-year-olds sitting there after midnight with a teddy bear between them was quite normal.

I opened my eyes. *Yes. The voice on the telephone belonged to Brother Phillip!*

I knew it with such certainty and with such a wave of fear for the way his voice had sounded during the evening's phone call that without thinking, I edged backward and sat on the edge of the bathtub for support.

In New York, Brother Phillip had become our lifeline of support during a nightmare as we discovered Joel had been kidnapped. He'd helped us until we finally found Joel. Was he in trouble now?

What had he said on the phone tonight?

"I . . . need . . . your . . . help. Find . . . me . . . at . . . the . . . end . . . of . . . circle. Remember . . . subway."

Remember the subway! How could I forget? When Joel had been lost beneath Manhattan, Brother Phillip had done what was needed to bring him back. And now he needed us.

I don't remember rinsing my mouth or getting ready for bed.

Later that night—I don't know how much later—I wandered out to our living room. There was something comforting about the easy chair, couch, and other familiar furniture draped in darkness. Comfort I needed more than sleep.

In the peace, I prayed. Or was it because I prayed that there seemed to be peace? You can't expect God to drop everything else He's doing and provide you with a miracle any time you have fears, but to know He's listening and that He cares makes a big difference when you're alone with troubles.

And I was definitely troubled.

It *had* been Brother Phillip pleading for help. I knew that as certainly as I knew my hands were clasped together in prayer.

But I knew little else. What kind of trouble? Why had he given a pizza order? And what about the sudden silence after a shout behind him?

I stood and moved to the front window. The moon edged past the top of our oak tree and cast silver light across the mid-November frost already heavy on the grass.

Brother Phillip had saved Joel's life. I smiled to remember my first impression of the man that night in the New York diner.

"Brother Phillip runs the mission down the block," Hugo said. *"He helps a lot of us street people get back to regular life."*

Us street people?

Hugo read my mind. "Brother Phillip got me my job here." Hugo grinned. "The Brother's not a bad guy for a preacher."

I stared. A preacher? In those old, almost tattered clothes? No haircut, no shave?

I was given little time to recover from that shock.

Mike elbowed me.

" . . . down at the street mission, someone might be able to help you," *Brother Phillip was saying. "A lost brother is a terrible thing."*

I looked at Brother Phillip more closely. His gentle eyes searched my face with compassion. How could I ever have doubted, even for a second, that this was a man of God? I reminded myself not to judge people by their appearances.

"Thank you, sir," I said.

His smile became grave. "But tell me, young man, how is it that you two are wandering the streets at this late hour? Despite that crazy bright shirt and mixed-up running shoes"—he grinned at Mike—"you're much too well dressed to be street people. Surely your parents must be worried about you, too, as well as the lost boy."

I continued to stare at the moonlight with unfocused eyes.

Something about Brother Phillip made you trust him immediately. That night Mike and I had explained to him everything about our desperate search for Joel, even how we had snuck out of our hotel room without permission to do so.

Brother Phillip had understood our fear and determination to find Joel before the worst happened.

Remembering all of it, it felt like yesterday, not half a year ago, that we had met.

After listening with obvious concern, Brother Phillip closed his eyes to think.

Finally he spoke again. "We have no right to hold you prisoner or interfere in any other way. Especially with your brother gone."

He paused to bite into his sandwich, then stopped as if a thought had hit, and placed it back on his plate.

"Okay," he said. "You keep looking. Meet me back at the street mission at six o'clock this morning. It's called The Good Shepherd's Corner. By then, some of the people will be awake. They'll be able to tell us if they saw Joel during the day. They'll also be able to help you look."

"An army of searchers!" Mike said.

Brother Phillip smiled. "Exactly. Until then, I want you protected."

He reached into his coat and pulled out a couple of graying business cards. On the front, each card had his name and the address of The Good Shepherd's Corner. He jotted something on the back and handed Mike the cards.

The words—we read later—instructed people in the area to extend us help in case of emergency, and that Brother Phillip personally guaranteed to be obliged for that help.

Mike grinned as he looked at the cards. "Thanks! What a break, running into you here!"

Brother Phillip's eyes twinkled. "Young man, if we both believed in only lucky breaks, it would be a sad, sad way to live."

Because his faith rested on more than lucky breaks, and because Brother Phillip's faith was obvious by how he helped those street people, his reputation on the streets had made those business cards a passport of safety for Mike and me.

Brother Phillip had done more than that, however—unseen things that finally brought us to Joel. And now he needed us.

But what could I do?

My jaw tightened in resolve. I could do as much as possible. Starting with those cards he had given us. They were in my closet, in a shoe box with other souvenirs. I got them.

Minutes later I tiptoed down the hallway from my bedroom.

"Dad," I said as quietly as possible when I reached the next doorway. His light snoring stopped immediately. "I know it's four in the morning, but I need to call New York."

CHAPTER 3

"There was no answer," I told Mike. "The number had been disconnected."

We were standing in my front yard. Mike had stopped by to pick me up on our way to school. The frost from the night before clung in patches to the remaining shade of the oak tree, and I kicked halfheartedly at clumps of leaves.

"Let me get this straight." Mike's blue eyes reflected sympathy. "One, a weird phone call has convinced you that Brother Phillip is in desperate trouble. Two, your dad didn't kill you for waking him up at four in the morning. Three, you actually asked him to call The Good Shepherd's Corner at that time. And four, because it's disconnected, you think we should cancel our Thanksgiving holiday plans."

I nodded, relieved at the understanding in his voice. "Exactly. I'm glad you're enough of a pal to see it my way."

"Mmmm." Mike scratched his chin. "Anything for a pal. Even if you think it's important enough to miss going to Disney World."

I nodded again. "It might be. Dad even called the police in New York to ask them to check the place. They said they'd call back. If something strange has happened ... well, we certainly owe Brother Phillip."

He shifted his school books from one hand to another. "Even if Ralphy and I have been saving for six months to go along with your family."

I kept nodding.

"Even if it means paying an extra twenty-five percent of our airfare to change flights."

I was starting to get dizzy from all my nodding.

"Even if it means facing gray, ugly New York weather instead of Florida sunshine."

"All of that, Mike."

Those words returned to my thoughts: *"Find ... me ... at ... the ... end ... of ... circle...."* *A long pause. The voice sounded hoarse with pain.* *"Remember ... subway."*

"Brother Phillip might be in trouble and we've got to help." I let out a deep breath of relief. "Here I was worried you might be upset."

"Naw." He ambled close to me and put an arm around my shoulder. "In fact, you know what?" I bent my head toward his as he lowered his voice to a confidential whisper. "I'm convinced of one thing."

"Yes?" I whispered back.

"You're totally crazy!" he shouted.

I fell backward with an eardrum rattled completely loose.

"One," he yelled as he glared down on me, "do you really think I'm stupid enough to fall for any of that? After last night, you'll do anything to play a trick on me."

The ground was cold and hard. I tried to move sideways, but Mike bent over and pushed my shoulders back.

"Change our Thanksgiving vacation," he snorted. "I'd rather put thumbtacks in my eyes. Hah!"

I tried plugging my ears, but it didn't help.

"Two, you may be convinced that the phone call was from Brother Phillip, but why should the rest of us stake a vacation on your imagination?" He paused to get air. "And three, even if it was Brother Phillip, what could we actually do to help him that would make it worthwhile for six people to throw away a trip to Disney World?!"

I lurched to my feet and mumbled something about how red hair can make people overreact.

"What's that?!" His voice rose even higher.

"Nothing." If I couldn't even convince my best friend that it was important to change a vacation, what chance did I have with my parents?

"Ricky," Mom interrupted from the front porch, "the New York police just called back. They left a message for you and your dad."

I held my breath as I walked closer.

"They explained why The Good Shepherd's Corner can't be reached." Her face showed worry. "It burned to the ground two days ago."

Mike's jaw dropped. "You're not playing along with one of Ricky's jokes, are you, Mrs. Kidd?"

"No," she said. "I wish I were."

"Brother Phillip?" I asked quickly. "Did they find him?"

She shook her head. Grim wrinkles tightened across her forehead. "No. He's been missing since then."

I gulped.

Mom's lips became thin lines of worry. "They did reach that Hugo fellow from the diner."

"Hugo!" Mike exclaimed as he remembered the huge gruff man who had been so kind to us.

Mom nodded. "Hugo. And it's not good news. Because he's afraid that Brother Phillip was trapped in the fire."

CHAPTER 4

"Don't let go of that teddy bear," Mom warned me. The noise of the crowd of people scrambling for luggage in the airport terminal forced her into a near yell. "If you do, we might well be looking for a *second* missing person."

Great. Holding a teddy bear was not my idea of the way to begin a search-and-rescue party.

We had less than five days—the rest of Thursday until Monday night. New York City contained nearly ten million people, and we had only four and a half days to find the single man who had once saved our lives. Yet my mother's first concern was for me to keep Joel's teddy bear in plain sight as a hostage so that he wouldn't disappear.

I grimaced sweetly. "Putting a choke hold on the bear now, Mom."

Dad spoke before she could reply. "Mike. Ralphy." He stood calmly amid all the swirling people. "Why don't you guys wade in there and find our luggage. We'll wait here so that we don't get separated."

"Yes, sir," they said together as they turned toward the baggage conveyor.

Despite being in New York instead of Orlando, Florida, despite the knot in my stomach that was from worry over Brother Phillip, I smiled as Ralphy's shirt flapped behind him.

No matter how hard Ralphy tried, his shirt always worked itself loose, probably because he was so skinny that he never could pull his belt tight enough.

I didn't know what excuse he could use for his hair. It stuck straight up in patches that no amount of gel could glue into place. Maybe his hair, like the rest of him, was a bundle of nerves.

That was our Ralphy. Computer genius and jumpy klutz. He'd be the one to get stuck in the Bradleys' fence with their German shepherds hot behind us in pursuit. But put him in front of a computer, and he became confident and strong.

Dad, of course, had no fear we'd lose sight of Mike or Ralphy. The blazing beacon of Mike's red hair and Ralphy's scarecrow appearance made them obvious a hundred yards away.

I thought sadly of our other friend, Lisa, who couldn't make this trip because her parents had planned a family reunion. It would have been nice to see more of her and maybe hear less wisecracking from Mike.

"You're fine, son?" Dad asked me as we waited. Mom, Dad, Joel, my baby sister, Rachel, and I formed an island in the sea of people moving from terminal to terminal.

"You mean, have I recovered from the heart attack Joel gave me this morning by hiding in my suitcase?" I asked. "Or am I still mad because he knocked my Thanksgiving dinner into my lap on the airplane? Or am I happy to have everybody staring at me because of the teddy bear in my left hand?"

Joel, who had his eyes riveted on the teddy bear, smiled at the mention of his favorite friend.

Dad chuckled. "No, I mean are you still worried about this change of plans. Remember, coming here wasn't just your decision. All of us agreed."

I nodded, but too slowly.

Dad rolled his eyeballs. "Do we have to go over all of it *again*?"

"No," I said. The police were convinced Brother Phillip had died in the fire. They refused to file a missing-person's report until the ruins had been completely searched.

But we knew by the phone call that he was alive. Plus, the possibility of arson had made us doubly suspicious. And Brother Phillip would never have called unless the trouble was deadly serious.

Mom caught the expression on my face and patted my shoulder to comfort me.

I didn't tell her about the doubts that were really on my mind. That phone call now seemed as if it had taken place a century earlier.

What if it hadn't been Brother Phillip? What if it *had* been a prank call? It was one thing to be sure at home, quite another to be sure here in New York. After spending so much time convincing the others it *was* Brother Phillip, I now wondered if I should have trusted my imagination.

There were two other things. The order for pizza, and the part about the end of the circle. To convince them all, I'd told them only that I knew the voice belonged to Brother Phillip. I hadn't said anything about those two things that now filled me with such doubt.

How could I now tell them I hardly believed myself anymore?

At two in the afternoon on Thursday, we reached The Good Shepherd's Corner in downtown Manhattan. And could only stare in silence for several minutes.

"Now I'm glad Mom wanted to relax at the hotel with Joel and Rachel," Dad finally said quietly. "To even think for a second that the man who saved your lives might have died there . . ."

I shuddered with him. The lead gray of a blustery November day pressed on us heavy enough. Seeing the blackened timbers of a building that had been completely gutted by fire was no way to be cheered.

"He's not in there," I said, more to convince myself than Dad, or Mike and Ralphy, who almost huddled together for comfort. "Brother Phillip is not dead."

Sure, I told myself. *But what if he had been in the building during the fire? How could he have survived? And, if he hadn't survived, how could that voice on the telephone have belonged to Brother Phillip?*

"It's so sad, isn't it?" Mike's face did not have the normal near grin that always made you suspect another trick. Instead, quiet thoughtfulness was easy to read.

"Yes." I knew what he was remembering. The building had once been much more than a small converted warehouse in a run-down neighborhood. It had been a home for street people. Brother Phillip's gentle strength had filled it with warmth and hope.

I remembered my first time inside. We had been so afraid for Joel, and Brother Phillip had eased that fear by telling us to come to the street mission for help. Walking inside, I could feel a difference by the way people moved. Their shoulders were straighter, chins higher than the poor people we had seen begging on street corners.

Now to see the bleak destruction in front of us filled me with sadness. I forced myself to remember how it once was, how I had seen it the first time.

The walls around us were gray with age. Faded posters of advertisements added some color. I guessed anything looked better than gray walls.

Above us on the second floor, Brother Phillip had explained, were rows of beds where the people slept. Around us, on the main floor, were long tables with folding chairs and a television corner with beat-up stuffed chairs and couches.

Across the main hall was a kitchen. In front were tables set up with plates and cups. We heard clanking and voices as people began to get breakfast ready.

Two rough-looking men joined us.

"Hey, dudes." The first man, short with greased-back hair, slouched as he greeted us and looked us over. "Cool bear, man," he said to me. "Wild shirt," he said to Mike and his Hawaiian pattern.

I'd been clutching Joel's bear for so long, I had forgotten it was there. Mike nodded appreciatively at the compliment about his shirt.

"Likewise, dudes." The second picked his teeth as he spoke.

He was black, tall and skinny, with hair in a tight Afro. "The Man here tells us you been looking for a runaway."

The Man? *The tall one answered my unspoken question.*

"Brother Phillip's cool. So cool some of us make it back to the real world. Like Hugo at the diner. Ain't nobody like Brother Phillip."

A gust of cold wind forced me to shiver.

Or at least I told myself it was the wind making me shiver, not wondering about where Brother Phillip was now. *He was a good man*, I told myself, *like the tall, skinny guy had said.* Then I realized with sudden horror that I had thought *was*, not *is*. Did I already believe Brother Phillip had died in the fire?

Another shiver made me tremble.

A hand on my shoulder broke through my thoughts.

"Brother Phillip must be as special as I've been led to believe," Dad said. "I look forward to meeting him."

Parents drive you nuts most of the time, but once in a while they read your mind and say exactly what you need to hear.

CHAPTER 5

At least walking down the streets of New York felt safer that day than it had in the spring when Mike and I were desperately searching for Joel. Now the sky was gloomier, the air colder, and the honking cars just as unfriendly, but this time we weren't without friends.

And each step took us closer to the diner and Hugo, the first friend we had made in the city.

"Just another block, Dad."

"Is this a race?"

His question caught me off guard. Then I realized what he meant as I heard Mike and Ralphy behind us puffing for breath. I was so anxious to get there, my walk had been almost a run.

I grinned sheepishly and made an effort to look around, as if we were tourists instead of people on a rescue mission.

The buckled pavement of the street reflected the neighborhood—old and well-worn. Low, flat buildings of gritty brick lined both sides of the street. Scraggly plants and sagging curtains showed apartment life on the second and third floors of each building. At street level, iron bars protected the display windows of the businesses. Faded billboard advertisements or cracked neon signs announced each storefront. "ROCK AND ROLL" BILLIARDS DOWNSTAIRS. MARTHA'S BUDGET FURNITURE.

JOE'S BURGERS—STEP INSIDE FOR COLD BEER AND HOT FOOD—CHEAP. FRED'S, WE PAWN ANYTHING.

Litter filled the sidewalks and gutters, and people hurried past us with their heads down against the wind. I was glad to live in a small town that had healthy trees instead of graffiti-filled street posts, and smiling familiar faces instead of cold-faced strangers.

"He'll make you order coffee," Mike was saying to Ralphy. "It's what Hugo told us the first time there." Mike lowered his voice to imitate Hugo. *"You wanna stay, you gotta be a patron, you wanna be a patron, you gotta order."*

Hearing that, I smiled. Hugo had appeared fierce the first time Mike and I stepped into the diner. The first thing we had noticed then was the jukebox playing, lonely in the early morning quiet.

"Yuck," Mike whispered. "Country music."

I whispered back. "Do you want to tell him you don't like his taste in music?"

Him was big. And mean-looking. Gray stubble on his face and a bristly crew cut. A dirty apron barely covered his solid belly as he stood behind the counter.

The glass door of the small diner closed behind us. Street lights shone in through large, streaked windows. The big man looked up at us and grunted.

"I'd never question his music," Mike said from the corner of his mouth. "I'm scared to even ask him about Joel."

That left the asking up to me. As we walked up to the counter, I said, "Excuse me, sir, we're looking for my brother, and I wonder if you could help."

"Coffee," he said. It didn't sound like a question.

"Pardon me?"

"Coffee. Are you drinking coffee."

"No, sir."

"Nobody stays in this diner unless they're patrons. Get it? Patrons. That means you eat or drink here. You wanna stay, you sit. You wanna sit, you order."

In the smile of remembering Hugo and how we choked down

terrible coffee, I almost forgot about the ache of worry for Brother Phillip.

That worry returned as soon as Mike opened the door of the diner. Like our first visit, we were here because of a desperate search. Nothing could make me forget that completely.

Country music greeted us. Again.

"Garth Brooks," Mike mumbled through a grin. "I've, uh, been listening to the country station at home. But don't tell anyone."

Hugo had his large back turned to us. He turned slowly as the door shut behind us. Same scowling face. Same bristly crew cut. Same solid belly and dirty apron.

His face showed no expression to see three boys and one father approach the line of stools in front of his counter.

He put his hands on his hips. "Is it coffee."

"Can a person qualify as a patron if he has a milk shake instead?" I did my best to hide any expression as I spoke.

"On one condition," he replied gruffly. "That the person doesn't pay for it." Then a massive grin broke through. "Ricky! Mike! And this must be Ralphy! It nearly killed me to keep a straight face." He leaned forward. "People expect that from someone as ugly as me, you know."

"That's why Mike never smiles," Ralphy said.

Mike elbowed him.

I ignored them. "Hugo, this is my father, Sam Kidd. Dad, this is Hugo, the guy I was telling you about."

"My pleasure," Hugo said as they shook hands. "Boy, I gotta tell you this is a great surprise, seeing ya here like this." His face darkened. "Ya heard about the fire."

We nodded.

"I hate to say it. But I gotta tell ya the same thing I told the cops. We're scared Brother Phillip never got out. It's been a couple days, and no one's seen him."

Dad spoke soberly. "I don't know if we have good or bad news, Hugo. That's why we're here."

Hugo wiped his hands against his apron, waiting for Dad.

"We're almost certain that Brother Phillip is still alive."

Hugo pounded the counter with a great ham fist. "That," he pounded the counter again to make his point, "is great news."

"Maybe not," Dad said. He explained the phone call.

"You're sure the call took place after the fire?" Hugo asked me. "You're sure it was his voice?"

I nodded, not trusting my voice to keep my doubts hidden.

"I gotta tell ya, if that's true, it's better than nothing. The street guys around here been in shock for the last couple of days. With Brother Phillip gone . . ."

Dad moved forward and took a seat on one of the round stools. "He sounds like a person whose actions were louder than his words."

Hugo started to say something, then stopped. "Let me get the milk shakes. A coffee for you, Sam?"

Five minutes later he had everything ready.

"Gimme another minute to take care of the other patrons, will ya?"

Soon Hugo was back. "Okay," he said firmly. "I just decided I can talk to ya about things I'd thought I'd say to no one else. Stuff I didn't tell the cops. Especially because we thought Brother Phillip really was gone."

Ice cream plopped onto the table from Ralphy's face. I nudged him and nodded at his chin so that he would wipe away the whipped cream that had smudged him from his milk shake. Ralphy wiped but only spread most of it across his cheek. I gave up and concentrated on Hugo's words.

"I think Brother Phillip was in trouble or something," Hugo said. "He was acting strange the few weeks before the fire."

Hugo wiped his hands again, even though they were clean.

"He just didn't seem to care like before. Someone would be in trouble and he'd just shrug. People would talk to him, and he'd forget to listen. I even heard—though I don't believe it—that some of the money donated to the mission had disappeared."

I shook my head. "Not Brother Phillip."

Hugo bit his lower lip and frowned. "That's what I said. But I also heard something else I didn't wanna believe." He paused, searching for the right words. "I'm told he took out a big insurance policy."

Our faces must have shown puzzlement.

"Fire insurance," Hugo said with a troubled voice. "Only a week before the fire. The cops found a gas can. The only reason people might believe the fire was an accident is because they figured he died in it. I mean, if you're trying to make money by burning your own building, would ya go back in to rescue people and kill yourself before you can spend a dime?"

All of our milk shakes stood in front of us, not even half gone.

"I've got a theory," Hugo continued. "Street people never ask anyone questions about their past. You wanna tell someone, fine, they'll listen. But they all mind their own business."

He shrugged. "We'd heard whispers about Brother Phillip's past. We didn't care much. The man was good. We all make mistakes, maybe he made his. But he looked out for people, and that was more than enough in this neighborhood."

Once again, all he saw on our faces was questions.

"Blackmail," Hugo said quietly. "All I can decide is someone knew something and was trying to force money from him. Someone who could bother the man so bad that his worry made him a different person. Made him lose his life in a fire he might have started himself."

He stopped and smiled a tight smile. "And now you're here telling me the man is still alive."

CHAPTER 6

By the time we finished our milk shakes, it was five in the afternoon. Effectively, that meant the end of day one of our search. That left less than four days to find Brother Phillip, and all we had managed to discover was that he was the main suspect in the arson that had devastated the street mission.

It didn't make me feel like dancing with joy.

I said as much to Mike and Ralphy as we followed Dad down the side street away from the diner.

"Me neither," Mike said. "I don't even know where to start next."

"Fire insurance," Dad said back over his shoulder without breaking stride.

"Good joke, Mr. Kidd." Mike kicked at a chocolate bar wrapper. "Except I don't own anything worth burning."

Dad's sigh was loud enough to reach us. "No, Mike. We find out who the fire insurance policy will benefit. If it wasn't Brother Phillip, we can start asking questions there."

Ralphy stumbled slightly as he tried tucking the tail of his shirt back under his jacket as he walked. "There's another thing," Ralphy blurted after recovering. "Brother Phillip's past. If we can prove there was nothing bad in it, we can prove he wasn't blackmailed. That way, at least, no one will ever think anything bad about Brother Phillip."

Three blocks remained before the subway entrance. Already the afternoon grew darker and the lights brighter. Continual honking of cars filled the background.

"Hold it," I ordered above the city noise. There must have been something in the tone of my voice. Even Dad stopped immediately and turned to face us.

"Please, please, please, don't talk about Brother Phillip as if he really is gone. He phoned for help"—I told myself as I spoke that there was no sense in doubting what I had so firmly believed following the phone call—"and we're here to do just that. Even if it seems impossible. That's all I have to say."

My face must have showed something, too. Because all they did was stare at me in silence, and I could feel my face tightening in determination.

That's when the mugging began.

Two guys stepped out from an alley. Hats pulled down low over their faces. Shoulder-length hair tied in ponytails. Scuffed leather jackets. Torn jeans. And each flicking a switchblade in deadly precision.

Three others—all in their late teens—walked up behind us to cut off any escape. Altogether, five scowling faces, five switchblades, and the slow, menacing movements of panthers closing in on helpless deer.

Our side street seemed isolated and lonely. The honking of horns from a main street just a block over reached us clearly, but with the gang members surrounding us, it was a world of distance away.

"Tourists," the leader sneered with a Hispanic accent when none of us made a sound. "Check out the dudes."

Dad stepped forward and shoved Ralphy, Mike, and me behind him.

"Ooooh. A tough guy," another one of the gang observed.

"Yeah, the old man thinks he's doing the kids a favor by blocking us out."

Laughter greeted that remark.

Dad said nothing, only put his arms out to keep the three of us behind him.

Then, in one swift movement, the leader stepped forward and thrust his switchblade at Dad!

My heart clutched.

Dad stood his ground and, with an equally swift move, chopped down with his right hand toward the wrist that held the slashing switchblade.

Both Dad and the leader missed their targets. The leader pulled his knife back out of reach so quickly I could hardly believe anything happened. And Dad's arm returned to a ready position.

"Not bad, man," the leader commented. " 'Specially for a tourist dude." He flipped the switchblade into the air and caught it by the blade. Then he extended the handle of it to Dad.

" 'Course," the leader said, "that's something we'd expect from the old man of Ricky Kidd." He motioned with the knife.

"Take this, please. You be with Ricky Kidd, you be part of our gang."

The leader of the gang pushed his hat up to clearly show his face. I rubbed my eyes.

"Whatsa matter, Ricky?" the leader continued. "You no recognize old friends?"

I shouted with glee. "The Vasquez Boys!"

Rocky Vasquez bowed gravely. "At your service."

"I knew it all along," Mike mumbled.

Rocky grinned a gleam of white. "Yeah, Mike? Then why you still holding Ralphy's hand?"

Mike looked down, dropped Ralphy's hand, looked up, and grinned back. "I was passing messages. We have a secret code. Two squeezes means get ready to attack."

"Good one, Mike," I said.

Dad said dryly, "I take it switchblades are the usual method of saying hello in this neighborhood."

Rocky shrugged with a shy smile.

"In Jamesville, we shake hands." Dad smiled back. "It tends to cut down on the number of heart attacks."

Dad stuck out his hand, and Rocky shook it. "Hello, Mr. Tourist. We heard you were here. Decided to look you up. Our way. Man, you guys be too easy to follow. Maybe you need lessons in smarts."

"How's Imalda?" I asked, to change the subject. Imalda was their younger sister, with all of them part of a large family that had been in as much trouble as Joel during our last visit to Manhattan. Without thinking, I rubbed my cheek in fond memory of how she had shown gratitude.

"That one," Rocky said as he rubbed his own cheek in imitation. "She still thinks about the kiss you be remembering right now."

I dropped my hand, glad that dusk concealed my flush of embarrassment.

"All of us, we always remember what you did to help us," he continued. "It's why we're here. You need something on the streets, we'll get it for you."

He paused. "Shame about your preacher friend. Brave. But not cool to go back in before the fire stopped."

"He's alive," I said. "And we'll take any help looking for him."

Rocky lifted an eyebrow in surprise. "You know something we don't?"

I explained the phone call and our conversation with Hugo. When I finished, Rocky spoke quickly in Spanish to his brothers. He then turned back to us.

"You got what we can give. The boys will be doing some asking, finding out if someone was leaning on the preacher, maybe how the leaning was done. We'll leave word with Hugo at the diner."

I nodded.

With a final salute, Rocky smiled, then spun on his heel. All of them melted back into the alley as silently as they had surrounded us.

"Ricky," Dad said as he let out a long breath and contemplated the switchblade in his hand, "after this, nothing about New York will come as a surprise."

He was wrong. That night around ten o'clock I answered a

knock on the door of our two-room hotel suite to find a man slowly pacing the hallway.

Just before the knock, all of us had been sharing the edge of a bed and watching television. Light from our room spilled into the hallway as I opened the door.

When the man looked up, it was another New York surprise that forced me to take a step back into the hotel room.

Deep dark circles under his eyes betrayed his exhaustion. His smile was weak and his first words were croaks that I couldn't understand.

But there was no mistaking him.

Brother Phillip.

CHAPTER 7

"Ricky?" That single word sounded full of hesitant relief, as if he couldn't believe it was me he finally saw.

"Brother Phillip!" I nearly hugged him, then remembered that Mike and Ralphy were behind me, so I coughed and offered my hand instead. "It's good to see you," I said formally.

He shook my hand. "It's good to see you, too. Hugo told me all of you were staying here."

Brother Phillip looked past my shoulder and smiled a wan smile. "Why don't you introduce me to everyone?"

I smacked my forehead in self-disgust. "Of course, please come in, it's just that it was such a surprise to see you and I'm forgetting my manners and . . ."

I stopped for breath, and Brother Phillip squeezed past me.

"Mom! Dad! This is Brother Phillip."

Mike and Ralphy rushed to meet him. They, too, caught themselves in time and went for the handshake instead of the hug.

Brother Phillip nodded gravely as he greeted them, then turned his attention to Mom and Dad.

"It's very nice to meet you, Mr. and Mrs. Kidd."

"Please," Dad said, "Stephanie and Sam. After all, we were on a first-name basis during our phone calls."

"Stephanie and Sam. It's very nice to finally meet you. In person."

"The pleasure is entirely ours," Mom said. She was holding my smiling little sister, Rachel, who looked adorable, as always, in a little pink outfit. "Especially after the way you helped out the boys when Joel was in trouble."

There was a small awkward silence as Brother Phillip looked modestly downward.

Mom filled it by speaking again. "Whatever's happened the last few days must have exhausted you. Please, sit down. We'll order you room service."

"That would be very nice," Brother Phillip said.

He moved to a chair and sat. He stood immediately.

"What the—! Oh. A teddy bear."

Joel appeared from beside the chair where he had been trying to do the *New York Times* crossword puzzle—in color. He had a red crayon tucked behind one ear.

"Yikes!" Brother Phillip jumped the way I had jumped thousands of times in my life.

"Joel," I admonished, "say hello to Brother Phillip."

Joel said nothing, only gazed upward.

Again an awkward silence.

"He's shy," Ralphy finally said. "And nervous about his teddy bear."

Brother Phillip tried a small smile, difficult by the tiredness so obvious on his face. He handed the teddy bear to Joel, who tucked it under his arm, then promptly pulled the red crayon from above his ear, parked a yellow crayon in its place, and returned to the crossword puzzle.

In the next moments of silence, I tried to compose myself amid the dozens of questions flooding my mind.

Where had Brother Phillip been? How had he escaped? Or had the phone call been my imagination after all?

Dad must have been reading my mind.

He coughed slightly to break the silence. "Brother Phillip. This is a very pleasant shock. Your phone call to Ricky left us, well, extremely worried."

Brother Phillip settled back in his chair and steepled his fingers beneath his chin. "Worried enough to change your vacation plans? Hugo told me. I'm sorry it happened that way. Sorrier than you can imagine, and I hope you can manage to forgive me. I don't have the money to—"

"To pay us back? That's silly," Mom said. "Money's not the issue. We knew you needed help. As Sam says, we're simply glad you no longer need it."

Or is Brother Phillip still in trouble?

"And," Mike said quickly, "we'll now have a lot of fun in New York knowing whatever forced you to call for help isn't forcing you anymore." Mike paused. "Right?"

That was Mike Andrews. As subtle as a train accident. But I squirmed with curiosity, too. *Why had Brother Phillip called? What had happened since to put him in this state of exhaustion? And*—I finally let the question slip through—*if he's here now, did it mean the fire at the street mission had not been an accident?*

Brother Phillip nodded. "Of course. You must have many questions. I'll try to answer them as best as possible. I'm wondering, however, if I might be bold enough to take you up on the offer of room service before I start."

Coffee and sandwiches arrived within five minutes. Another five minutes passed while Brother Phillip ate.

I tried not to stare while we waited. His hair was clumped and matted and longer than I remembered from before. His beard, which had been glossy dark with health on our first visit, now seemed sparser and lighter. His eyes no longer glowed with obvious and gentle strength.

Yet this was the man who had given so much hope and comfort to the desperate street people, and who had been compassionate without judging. As he finished his second cup of coffee, I remembered what he had told me as I stood near the kitchen of the street mission during our previous search for Joel.

Brother Phillip returned and noticed my stares of curiosity and pity. A cloud of pain crossed his face as he explained the lives of the people around me.

"If we could do more," he said, "some of these people wouldn't have to go out on the streets. Unfortunately, all we can do is give them a place to sleep and barely enough food to get by. They go out during the day and come back nights when they feel like it or when it gets too cold. Some work odd jobs or shine shoes and clean car windows, but some of them are forced to look in garbage cans for bottles or any junk they might sell. Others beg, and, I'm afraid to say, still others steal."

I spoke in a low voice to keep the rough-looking men down the table from hearing. "But how can you let people in if you know they're going out there to steal?"

Brother Phillip shook his head sadly. "At best, we let them know what's right and what's wrong, but we don't push it. Too many questions or too much preaching, and they won't come here for help. And they need it so badly, we don't have the luxury of choosing who's good or bad."

Brother Phillip smiled. "Besides, if God decided to help only the people who deserved it, none of us would pass the test."

A clank of china took me from my thoughts. Brother Phillip had drained the last of the coffee, then set the cup down on the tray.

He rubbed his face with both hands, took a deep breath, then spoke.

"In answer to your question, Mike, no, I don't need help any longer." Brother Phillip searched all of our faces. "In fact, I never did."

We waited.

"It's been a long, long time since the Gulf War," he said. "But I still have flashbacks. The fire, well, it freaked me out. I thought I was there again, with the flamethrowers, the roaring of shells exploding, all of that."

He groaned slightly. "It's terrible to suddenly find yourself there. And so believable. I . . . I . . . don't remember much after the first flames licked through the doorway. Hugo tells me I went back in, but for me, nothing. I don't remember that, or coming out."

His smile was bleak. "I can barely remember calling you, Ricky. In the fog that surrounded me, all I wanted was survival, a way out. You guys are all good memories for me. Not bad like the horror of my flashback. I must have subconsciously cried out for you, then in my daze actually made the phone call."

Brother Phillip spread his hands helplessly. "This morning I woke up on a park bench. I didn't even know which day it was. And when I got to the street mission, it was gone. Charred wood and crumbled bricks." He swallowed several times to regain control of his voice. "Hugo had to tell me what happened. And as soon as I heard you were here, I knew I had to let you know I was fine."

He searched our faces again. "Honest. I'm just fine."

If only that had been the truth.

CHAPTER  8

I woke Friday morning to a suffocating blackness.

"Ummphh!" I flailed my arms to fight for oxygen.

"Ummmmph!" My hands found what I expected. I pushed a certain someone away from the bed and yanked the pillow from my face.

"Joel," I hissed. "I've told you a million times not to do that."

"You wouldn't talk," Joel accused.

He carefully measured the distance between us for safety. Sometimes when he wakes me that way, I don't react too calmly. In this case, I knew Mom and Dad were in the other room of our hotel suite. In other words, discretion was a necessity.

"It's true, Ricky." Mike smirked from his bed as he leaned on his elbow. "He asked you five times for a dollar and you kept snoring."

"One, I don't believe I snore. Two, why didn't you stop him?"

"Because I'd never seen his famous pillow-stuffing alarm clock trick in real life. It was pretty neat, wasn't it, Ralphy?"

"Definitely." Ralphy nodded his head rapidly. He rubbed his eyes and sat up in his pullout sofa bed. "First Ricky twitched a bit. Then, flip-flop, he started squirming like a fish out of water."

"Hah, hah. You guys try living with a kid brother like Joel."

"I need a dollar," Joel said.

"That makes six times." Mike smirked again. "I'd say he wants it pretty bad."

I groaned. "It's only seven-thirty, Mike. Why would he need a dollar?"

Joel ignored my ignoring him, and kept his distance. "I need a dollar for the soda machine."

Mike giggled. "He's your brother, pal."

"It's bad for his teeth and it'll spoil his breakfast."

"So now you're his mother?" You can always tell who's a good friend. He's the one loving it most when you're having a hard time.

"Fine," I grumped. I pulled a pair of jeans from the floor, dug the wallet loose from the back pocket, and pulled a five-dollar bill loose for Joel.

"Hey!" Mike yelped in sudden realization. "Those were my pants!"

"Imagine my making a mistake like that." I watched with satisfaction as Joel reached the door. "And there he is. Already gone."

I closed my eyes to Mike's complaining.

Naturally, just as I was about to fall asleep, a knock on the door pulled me from my drowsiness.

"Joel forgot his key," I mumbled to Ralphy. "Can you get the door?"

"Sure." Ralphy hopped out of the sofa bed.

"Nice legs, Ralphy," Mike said from his bed. "Steal them from a chicken?"

"Very funny." Ralphy wore an extra-large T-shirt instead of pajamas, one that nearly reached his knees. His legs were all bone and skin, and what wasn't knobby was very thin, and everything was white enough to blind you at any time of day, let alone this early in the morning.

He yawned and opened the door. Then froze with one hand still stretched high in the middle of his yawn.

"Move queeckly! All of you!" said the person at the door.

Imalda Vasquez! As solemnly pretty as I remembered. Long black hair. High, delicate cheekbones. Dusky skin. The girl who had given me a kiss of gratitude that could still make my cheek burn in memory.

By the urgency on her face, I doubt she noticed Ralphy was not fully dressed. Ralphy thought the opposite.

"Eeeeep!" Jarred out of paralysis by her voice, Ralphy jumped at least a foot and landed facing the opposite direction in a full sprint. White legs flashed in all directions as he scrambled for the covers of his sofa bed.

The bed *boinged* under the impact of his full dive, groaned once, then folded shut on Ralphy with a slow and majestic sigh.

"Imalda—" I began. But not until I had pulled my covers up to my chin.

"You must get dressed. All of you. Your brother's been kidnapped!"

She spun around and closed the door behind her.

"It's a joke, right?" Mike said. "Just like the mugging yesterday."

I shook my head. "She sounded too scared."

Instead of arguing further, I jammed on my blue jeans, pulled a T-shirt over my head, and slapped bare feet into my sneakers.

Mike dressed himself almost as instantly.

A small wheezing reminded us of someone else. It came from the folded-up bed. Only a pair of feet stuck out.

"Nuts," I said. "You help Ralphy. I'll talk to Imalda."

Without looking back, I moved to the door.

She was waiting directly in front, pacing nervously.

"We were watching your room," she said. "Waiting for the time to wake you. Joel, he came out, so my brother and I followed. Then it happened. At the soda machine. The man grabbed him and—"

Mike and Ralphy flung open the door.

I gripped her arm. "Where did they go?"

"I watched the elevator. It went to P. The parkade." She was already half running down the hallway to the stairs. She called over her shoulder, "I don't know if my brothers made it there in time."

We found Joel playing with a switchblade.

"It's okay," Rocky Vasquez called as we rounded the corner of the elevator room to hit the parkade at full sprint. "We got the kid."

Rocky and two Vasquez brothers stood around Joel, glancing beneath the dim underground lights to scan the silent cars for movement. They seemed unconcerned about the razor-sharp knife in his hands.

Within seconds we were close enough to see Joel clearly. As I walked, trembling from a mixture of fear, anger, and excitement, Joel popped the switch, then smiled as the blade flicked free of the handle. He worked his tiny fingers around the back edge of the blade, pushed it back into the handle, then searched again for the release button.

"Joel," I said crossly as I stepped among the brothers, "you'll hurt yourself."

He shrugged, then handed me the switchblade.

"The guy stepped on his teddy bear," Rocky apologized. "I thought I'd give him something to make up for it."

I tried not to let my frustration show. "A can of soda's better for him."

"We, uh, drank it," one brother said. "All that running made us thirsty. We kept the can. Like, for if you want the deposit or anything."

I shook my head.

Mike asked the obvious question. "What happened?"

Rocky pursed his lips. "This whole thing's too strange."

Something dawned on me. "Why would you be guarding our room so early?" Then I asked the more obvious question. "Why would anyone kidnap Joel? And who?"

Rocky dropped his voice to a whisper. "It's this fire thing. Last night we asked around the streets. Then within an hour we got warned off by some bad dudes. Made us mucho nervous. So we figured this game's bigger than you could guess. Thought it wouldn't hurt to be invisible, but guard your room in case something happened." Rocky smacked a fist into his palm.

"Then, just like that, someone yanked the kid, teddy bear, can of soda and all, and hit the elevator. Three of us chased him, going down the stairs, taking turns stopping at each floor to make sure he don't get off the elevator. Soon as he spots us in the parkade, he drops the kid and is gone. Like, I ain't seen nobody move the way that guy did. He's All-Pro if he's anything."

It was too much too quickly for me. "Hang on. You think someone's out to get us because we're asking questions about Brother Phillip? That Joel was snatched because—"

I was able to say no more.

"Hey! You! What're you kids doing there!"

A boulder-bellied security officer waddled toward us, waving a billy club.

"The diner," Rocky hissed. "Meet us at Hugo's diner in an hour. Don't get your old man or old lady involved. Not till you know more."

I looked at him blankly.

"I said, 'HEY YOU!'" The security officer's red face blustered rage.

"Alone," Rocky hissed. "Meet us there alone."

The four of them—Imalda included—wheeled away as if one person. Within seconds they were only shadows.

"We're hotel guests," Mike said politely as the security guard waddled into conversational range. "We can show you our keys." He held his up as proof.

I remembered the switchblade in my hand. I slipped it into my rear pocket to hide it from the guard, then bit down hard to keep sudden agony from escaping my mouth.

I kept my hand in my back pocket as the guard glared at us. "Friends of yours?"

"They were just going to ask us something when you shouted," Mike replied. "Maybe it was a good thing you stopped by. They didn't look too friendly, did they?"

The guard stared at us for long moments, then grunted. "Watch yourselves. This town ain't great for dumb tourists."

He hitched his belly over his belt, then waddled back to the parkade entrance.

When it was safe, I let out a long breath of pain and removed my hand from my pocket.

"He was saying," Mike observed mildly, "something about dumb tourists?"

We all watched small drops of blood splatter onto the concrete of the parking lot. Unfortunately, I had worse things to worry about than the two fingers so recently slashed by a switchblade popping free in my pocket at the wrong time.

CHAPTER 9

"Stephanie," Dad said during our discussion in the hotel room a half hour later, "they'll be in good hands."

"How can you say that? This is New York. Someone just tried to kidnap Joel. Ricky nearly cut his fingers off"— I winced at her exaggeration—"and now you want me to trust the three of them to a street gang?"

I had not even been tempted to remain silent about the beginning of our day. Even though Rocky had warned us not to involve the grown-ups, there was no way I wanted to avoid it. So we had described everything and ended by asking Mom and Dad to let us go to the diner. Alone.

"I have a suspicion," Dad said wryly, "that the Vasquez Boys are the best protection going."

"What kind of influence will they be on the boys?"

"Perhaps Ricky and Mike and Ralphy might be an influence on them."

Mom half smiled at that. She tried her last card. "But look what Ricky did to his fingers. With *their* switchblade."

I winced, remembering how much the iodine from an old hotel first-aid kit had stung.

"He'll promise not to touch it again. Not until he learns to be smart." Dad placed his hand on her shoulders. "You and I will have Rachel and Joel. We'll look into finding out who benefited from the fire insurance. The boys will listen to the Vasquez boys for information on the blackmailer. That's it. Then they'll return. After all, you have to agree that Brother Phillip did not look well last night. We can't merely do nothing."

Mom stared at him for nearly a minute.

"Sam," she said, "you're so cute with that stubborn look in your eyes."

Dad blushed.

My watch showed 9:05.

Mike, Ralphy, and I sat on the round stools at the counter, contemplating the coffees we had insisted on ordering to qualify as patrons. We spun around when Rocky walked into the diner and past the few people at tables.

I kept my bandaged fingers out of sight.

Rocky squinted in the direction of the jukebox. "Hey, Hugo. When you gonna play some real music? Every time I walk in, I look for horses, man."

Hugo rested his ham-like arms on the counter and growled as he leaned between Mike and me to scowl at Rocky. "You saying you don't like country music?"

Rocky winked at us. "I'm saying it belongs in Montana, not New York City."

Hugo growled again. "I get enough headaches in New York. I don't need your kinda music for more. That stuff, pal, their screaming sounds like they slammed their fingers in a door."

Rocky shrugged before throwing a leg over the stool beside me. "Next you'll be telling me I need a haircut?"

"Nah," Hugo said. "Next I'll be telling ya to order. You wanna stay, you gotta be a patron, you wanna be a patron—"

Rocky sighed a large theatrical sigh. "I know the rules. I'll take a cup of that acid you call coffee."

"Acid?" Ralphy asked. "But I thought—"

Mike elbowed him. That's the thing about computer geniuses; they sometimes can't figure out when people aren't serious.

"Hugo," Rocky said in a quieter, more respectful tone of voice, "if ya got a few minutes, I wouldn't mind you listening in on this. It's about Brother Phillip."

"You got it, Rocky. Give me a few seconds to check on the other patrons."

"Rocky," I whispered, "where are your brothers? I thought we were meeting all of you."

He grinned. "You mean, 'Where's Imalda?'"

My turn for a large theatrical sigh.

Rocky's face became serious again. "All of them are outside, watching from hiding spots. We're jumpy on this one. It don't hurt to be cautious."

Hugo returned. "You guys know Brother Phillip was here last night."

It was a statement.

"Yes." Mike nodded. "Thanks for sending him by the hotel."

"Not a problem. He said he was going to the cops today to straighten everything out. Tell them about the flashback and all." His large face crinkled with worry. "But it still don't explain the fire or the way he's been acting."

Rocky became almost rigid. "Cool it on that fire stuff, Hugo. I don't want to see you get hurt."

Hugo snorted, then looked down at his broad arms folded across his chest. "Nobody hurts Hugo."

Rocky tightened his lips. "Benito hurts anyone, man. Even someone as big as Hugo."

"Benito the Bookie?" Hugo's voice could barely be heard.

Rocky nodded. "That's why I want all of you listening good."

I forgot all about trying to choke down my coffee.

"We put our ear to the streets last night. I already told you that. What we first hear ain't good. Brother Phillip's into Benito the Bookie for a hundred."

Rocky caught the puzzled look on Ralphy's face. "Bookie. That's a guy who takes illegal bets. Horse races, football games, basketball, baseball. Anything. He gives you odds and you bet. But with Benito, you don't want to be owing for long."

"Benito." Hugo's face became grimmer. "He's got heavy connections. Heavy backers."

Rocky nodded again.

"So Brother Phillip owes Benito a hundred," Mike said. "That's no big deal. We'll pitch in and help him out of the jam."

I was watching Rocky very carefully. My stomach turned to ice.

"Mike," I said, "I don't think Rocky meant a hundred dollars."

Rocky confirmed it for me. "A hundred grand, Mike. Brother Phillip's into Benito for a hundred thousand dollars. And we heard something else, too."

Rocky sipped once from his plain white coffee mug. "Brother Phillip could get the money in a second. From his family. To them, a hundred grand ain't much more than a sneeze."

Rocky shrugged. "So there's another question. Why don't Brother Phillip go to his old man if Benito the Bookie's ready to kill him?"

CHAPTER 10

"Take your hat off, Mike. You can leave it here with Hugo."

"My hat? But—"

Rocky held out his hand. "Your hat. The way you look is gonna be real important."

"My hat? But—"

"Mike, I'm eighteen. I been around. I know these things. That's why you guys are going and the Vasquez Boys will just wait down the road. Out of sight."

"That's unfair," I protested. "If you're polite and ask nicely then you should be able to go there just as well as any of us."

For the first time, Rocky's face showed sadness instead of toughness. He held his hands open and away from his body. "Look at me," he said. "Take away the hair, put me in a suit, maybe I got a chance to talk to people who live in a mansion by the river. But not much of a chance. Suit and a good haircut don't make my skin creamy white like theirs. I open my mouth, they know I'm some Hispanic kid who ain't been to school. And they're gonna know I don't belong in their territory. Just like they know they don't belong in mine."

He shifted from foot to foot. I suddenly realized he was almost afraid of standing inside the mansion at the river, as afraid as Brother Phillip's parents would be on a dark street in downtown New York.

"So this is the deal," Rocky continued. "You guys look nice, the way they expect people in their world to look. Mike takes off his hat, combs his hair neat, and keeps his crazy Hawaiian shirt hidden beneath his jacket, he'll pass as a respectable kid from a good background. They'll talk to you. And that's what we need. More information from them millionaire parents of his."

Mike slowly removed his baseball cap, handed it to Hugo, and ran his fingers through his hair.

I don't know what distracted me more. The dollars clicking with each passing mile on the taxi meter, or having Imalda so close beside me in the backseat.

I tried not to remember our final meeting the time before in New York, but of course the more I tried not to remember it, the more it ran through my thoughts.

"Reeecky, thank you so much," she said. "I, Imalda Vasquez, thank you on behalf of my entire family."

She was nearly as tall as I was. Which was confirmed when she gave me a hug and kissed my cheek. This kissing business was addictive.

"Oh, we do this sort of thing all the time," I replied when she let go. People have to act cool around good-looking girls. It's part of the rules, isn't it?

Imalda giggled. "Sure. That's why you and your friend hold hands with a teddy bear in the middle of Central Park."

Oops. I'd forgotten about that.

When she interrupted my thoughts, it was with the same voice I was remembering so vividly. So for a moment I didn't realize that she, not her memory, was speaking.

"I said," she added with a poke in my side, "don' you be worrying about cab fare. The Vasquez family owes you much more than that."

"But," I whispered back, "it's been a half hour. By the time we get back to Manhattan, it'll be a fortune."

She leaned her face to my ear, close enough that I felt the warmth of her breath. "Shhhh," she said softly. "I wanna hear no more."

Mike grinned at my red face.

So I took advantage of having the window seat and concentrated on the *outside* scenery.

It had taken fifteen minutes—and forty dollars on the meter—to reach Interstate 87. Our cab had jostled for position at seventy miles an hour on that crowded six-lane, going north to the Highway 9 exit, then turned off that highway ten minutes later. The blur of concrete and brick and glass and steel and traffic lights had gradually dissolved to older, stately houses, and now, as the cab wound its way down to the Hudson River, the houses progressed larger and larger in size, half hidden by cultivated hedges and towering trees.

The stubbly-faced cab driver raised his voice above the various rattles of his old taxi. "Hey, you guys want me waiting, I'm gonna need more deposit money. This meter don't stop running when the car does."

Rocky unfolded more money and silently handed it across.

The cab driver wiped a free hand over his half-bald head and grunted in satisfaction. "You guys know we're getting into some kind of ritzy area."

"Yeah," Anthony, another Vasquez, muttered.

"So what I'm saying," the cab driver continued, "and it's strictly for your benefit, is that chances are down by the river them houses will have gates."

"Yeah," Anthony muttered again.

"So if you catch my drift, what I'm trying to tell ya is that unless you got a good reason, the closest you're gonna get to the house is the front gate."

"Yeah."

The cab driver shrugged. "As long as you know. It's your money you'll be wasting."

We reached the end of a plateau in the road, and curves of the pavement drew us downward toward the Hudson River. The cab driver had been right; most of the houses did have front gates and a tiny guardhouse.

How will we get past the gate to speak to these rich people?

It saddened me to realize Rocky had been accurate about his unlikely chances of convincing someone to let him reach Brother Phillip's parents. Money was a cruel and cold barrier.

Before I could puzzle over that, two things happened.

The cab driver stopped in front of an imposing brick wall twenty yards down from another driveway entrance. And turned to tell us that someone was following us.

CHAPTER 11

"This is weird anyway, a bunch of kids like you taking a joyride to this area," he complained. "And the cab behind us has been there long enough to finally make me nervous."

Before I could crane my neck to get a look, the cab zoomed past us. With no passengers.

"Relax, man," Rocky, in the front with Anthony, instructed our driver. "Ain't nobody in there."

Our driver shrugged. "Whatever you say, bud. Just trying to help."

Rocky squirmed to look at Mike and Ralphy and me, crammed in the backseat with Imalda.

"Anthony and I'll wait here with the taxi. The rest is up to the four of you. You know the questions to ask."

"What if the guard at the gate doesn't let us through?" Mike asked.

"Be charming, Mike," I said. "Just be charming."

"Mr. DuBerg says he's afraid it is not convenient to see visitors at this time."

The guard's face and voice matched the rest of him. Bland perfection. Neatly pressed gray uniform. Short, brushed hair. And a lack of expression that verged on boredom.

"Sir, we've come a long way." Mike flashed a grin that would have earned him two dozen cookies from any of the old ladies back in Jamesville.

"I'm sorry if I didn't make myself clear," the guard said. "You may have flown in by private jet from China and it still would make no difference. The DuBerg family is *not* receiving visitors."

Mike's grin dimmed to a four-cookie level.

"Let's go," Imalda said with a slight falter in her voice. "We've already been here too long."

She must be as conscious of the status difference as Rocky, I thought; *her mask of coolness is growing visibly tight.*

Naturally, I was stupid enough not to be scared.

"Will you repeat to Mr. and Mrs. DuBerg," I asked, "that this relates to their son, Phillip." Inspiration hit as I realized that since they had the money to buy anything they wanted, what must be valuable was something they couldn't buy. More privacy.

"And," I continued, "will you please tell them that we are trying to spare them any bad publicity regarding their son's actions."

The guard blinked. Twice. I must have made an impression.

He wheeled back into the guardhouse without speaking, then spoke quietly into a telephone.

"You will be received now," the guard said on his return.

Within minutes the gate slid back on well-oiled hinges. A limousine glided down the long driveway in our direction.

The chauffeur's only acknowledgement of our presence was a slight nod as he held open the back door.

"Check this out, pal. Television, car phone, and fax machine," Mike whispered to me in the hushed luxury of the wide backseat.

I did not. My last words to the guard were haunting me. *We are trying to spare them any bad publicity regarding their son's actions.* Did that mean a part of me already believed Brother Phillip had set fire to his own street mission?

The hushed drive lasted nearly a minute as the ⟨ directed the limo like a cruise ship. When he stop[bered to wait until he opened the back door for us.

Ralphy gaped at the mansion. "It's as big as a h⟨

Imalda bit a fingernail. "I told Rocky not to sen⟨ tered. "But no, he said a girl would make them feel able. Easy for him to forget what I might feel."

I tried manly comfort. "You'll be more beautiful in the house."

She thought for a moment, then smiled me a s⟨ getting the strange looks from Ralphy and Mike mo while.

The chauffeur led us up marble steps as wide as a Huge, elaborately carved wood doors swung open.

"Of course," Mike whispered. "The butler."

He was dressed in a long-tailed jacket and manag⟨ his lips as he spoke. "This way, if you will."

His shoes clicked each step down a long corridor l ens of oil paintings.

He pushed another door open and held it for us. library. The butler retreated. Ralphy blurted, "This i our school's!"

Shelves of rich, dark wood—filled to the ceiling w books—completely lined each wall. And yes, there knight's armor in the corner.

A man and woman stood at the library window, large expanse of lawn. When they turned to face us, streaming from behind them cast their features in dark

Words reached us from the silhouette of the man. he stated flatly. "It's blackmail."

CHAPTER 12

He stepped away from the sunlight and I saw his face clearly. Thin and scornful.

"Blackmail?" I repeated.

"Yes, blackmail. Threatening us with bad publicity. I would call that blackmail." He paused and treated all of us to a cold smile. "You have thirty seconds."

I should have been very scared. Instead, I became angry, the good kind of angry that fills you when you know you are in the right, the kind of angry that somehow instinctively tells you what to do.

Instinct told me to smile back at the man.

"My name is Ricky Kidd, sir. These are my friends. Imalda Vasquez. Ralphy Zee. Mike Andrews."

"Twenty seconds."

"Except for Imalda, who lives in downtown New York, we're visiting from a small town called Jamesville. For the second time in less than a year."

"Ten seconds."

"Our first time in New York," I said, "we met a man whose parents should have no reason to be blackmailed. Because although his parents were very wealthy, Brother Phillip worked for poor people in downtown New York. He also helped save our lives."

"Your time is—" The man stopped as if I had slapped

him on the cheek. "You said . . . *Brother* Phillip."

I nodded. Mr. DuBerg seemed to slowly fold as he reached for a plush, deep chair beside him. The woman moved with him and stood beside the chair with her hand on his shoulder.

With the scorn drained from his face, he suddenly looked old and frail. It emphasized an age difference between them that grew every second.

She wore a simple black dress that at first had made her seem middle-aged. As I looked closer, I saw she wasn't much older than my mother, with short brunette hair and little makeup.

He was dressed as if he had stepped out of a men's fashion magazine. But when you looked past the clothing, you realized he was probably in his early sixties.

"Brother Phillip," he repeated slowly.

A strange light of new strength began to glow in his eyes. "Perhaps not all your news of my long-lost son is bad."

CHAPTER 13

Mr. DuBerg smiled ruefully. "You are right, of course, to introduce yourself first. Please accept my apologies for forgetting my own manners. It's just that news of my son was so ... so ..."

Then he frowned. "But you did hint that the news might be bad."

"Henry," the woman beside him said in a low voice. "The introduction."

"Yes. Yes. Please allow me. I am, as you might know, Henry DuBerg. The Third, if that makes a difference. Henry One and Henry Two painstakingly built a fortune in the manufacturing business, so large that my entire life has been spent maintaining it."

The woman coughed discreetly.

"And this"—he motioned gracefully to the woman standing beside him—"is my daughter-in-law, Joan Du-Berg. Her husband, Phillip's older brother, is in Europe on business, and she has been kind enough to visit during his absence."

She came forward and shook all of our hands, saving a special warm smile for Imalda, who could not escape discomfort in the presence of a woman who probably had more money in jewelry around her neck than the entire Vasquez family might earn in a lifetime.

"Young Master Kidd," said Mr. DuBerg, "I am anxious to hear what you know about Phillip. However, too many years among the sharks of this world has convinced me that when people come visiting, it is rarely to give but to receive. Before I ask you for information, please tell me what it is you want."

"To know more about Brother Phillip. We're trying to help him."

"Ah, good. We will be able to make a fair exchange." He looked upward at Joan DuBerg. "Please, dear, will you ring for tea." He paused. "Also, please inform security it will not be necessary for the police to detain the taxi that is waiting for these young people." He smiled at our startled glances. "Security cameras along the wall."

Joan slipped quietly from the room.

"Please, Master Kidd," he said as the door closed without a sound, "tell me everything you know about my son Phillip."

I did. I started with the first time Brother Phillip and I had met in Hugo's diner. Then explained how street people had seemed at peace in Brother Phillip's gentle presence. How he had been so crucial to saving our lives.

Halfway through, Joan returned as quietly as she had left. She listened as attentively as her father-in-law.

I told how some of Brother Phillip's answers had helped me with my own struggles during our first visit to New York. And then finished with the bad news—everything that had led to our second visit, right to the taxi that now waited outside the mansion's gates.

Mr. DuBerg closed his eyes in thought.

The butler entered the library, pushing in a silver tea tray. He served all of us in silence.

That was something about being very, very rich that I had never considered. How immense wealth wrapped them in a silence that was so far away from the good-natured bickering of my house or Ralphy's or Mike's, and even farther away from the sirens and blaring horns that surrounded Imalda all her life.

I noticed that Imalda did not start sipping her tea immediately.

Instead, she watched Joan with a careful eye and then imitated the older woman's manners.

Mike, on the other hand, clanked his spoon with great enthusiasm as he stirred milk and sugar into his cup. He grinned appreciation at the stack of cookies on a silver platter and beat Ralphy there by a split second.

"You have been most candid," Mr. DuBerg said when the butler departed and left us the tray. "I shall do the same, although, as you will see, it is not a prospect that I relish."

As he stared at the far wall of the library, he mused, "My deepest regret is that I did not forgive him."

Then he focused his eyes sharply on us. "I loved Phillip as deeply as any man could love his own son. He was bright, cheerful, and always treated his mother—God rest her soul—and me with great respect and love in return. I suppose that's why it hurt so badly when he changed."

"Sir," I said very quietly, "as any man could love his own son? I'm not sure I understand."

He took a breath. "Phillip was adopted. I wish . . ."

He hesitated, then gave a weak smile. "Funny, I had no problem telling you. But with Phillip, it was something we decided to tell him when he was older. And the right day never seemed to come."

Another weak smile. "Now I have to wonder if it would have made a difference."

He didn't explain further, and I didn't press him for an answer.

His hand trembled as he reached to replace his cup on the tray. "I presume," he interrupted himself with a trace of irony, "that all the cookies met your requirements."

Mike and Ralphy wiped crumbs from their cheeks and nodded.

"They're from a special German recipe. Something in which our cook takes great pride."

I ignored the empty tray. The story had kept me from eating more than one cookie anyway, and I wanted him to continue.

After a sigh, he did. "It was his second year in college. Disturbing stories about his activities there reached us. Misbehavior I could hardly believe. The details, I'd rather not repeat. When I went to the college to confront him, he neither denied nor confirmed it, just retreated with a distant quietness that made me feel like I wasn't even part of his life. Despite that, upon leaving his room that day, I was still determined to love him."

There came a long pause. The sun broke through some clouds, casting a sudden beam into the library that etched a sharp shadow over the back of his chair.

His voice seemed to grow darker, as well. "Only two weeks later I came home early from a business trip. Unexpected, I'm sure, because as I went upstairs, I caught a glimpse of him hurrying from my study into his bedroom. I thought nothing of it, calmly said hello, and continued to my own bedroom to make some private calls as the luggage was being brought up. When I finished, Phillip had already left. And that night I banished him from this house and from my heart."

The old man struggled forward from the depths of his plush chair. Joan lent him an arm and he stood, then walked in dignified silence to the window and stared over his property.

When he spoke again, I realized why. He did not want us to see his face. But his breaking voice betrayed his emotions.

"My study, you understand, contained until that day what had been one of the premier stamp collections in the United States. After discovering Phillip was no longer in the house, I discovered neither were ten of the most valuable stamps in the collection."

His shoulders slumped. "Phillip returned that night as if nothing had happened. How can you arrest your own son? Instead, I gave him the chance to confess, to return the stamps. He did not. So, I gave him an hour to pack as many of his belongings as he could into his car. Then I forbade his presence in my life again."

Mr. DuBerg faced us. He squared the shoulders of his navy blue suit jacket, defying us to see any weakness in the tears streaming down his cheeks.

"So there you have it. If someone is blackmailing Phillip, you know exactly why. Two million dollars in stolen rare stamps."

CHAPTER 14

It was noon that Friday by the time we got back to the hotel.

Dad merely raised an eyebrow at our entrance. "Long discussion at the diner?"

I shook my head. "The Vasquez Boys took us on a detour. Tell them, Ralphy," I said.

He did. He might have been tongue-tied with awe at the mansion, but as soon as we had gotten into the cab, he'd blabbed and blabbed about it for miles.

"It was, like, so, well, like, oh, Mike, why don't you tell them."

Nothing like the spotlight of attention to make Ralphy blush and forget anything he was about to say.

Mike explained everything instead.

"Don't forget to tell them about the cookies," I reminded him.

"The best," he said fervently. "Absolutely the best."

Since he missed my sarcasm the first time, I tried again. "And tell them how you ate every one."

"With Ralphy's help. He had about half."

There was a quick tug on my pants leg.

I jumped.

"Joel," I hissed when my heart found its way back into my chest. "Give me a warning before you show up."

"That *was* my warning."

"Fine. What do you want?"

"Cookies."

"Maybe later. You *do* remember Brother Phillip, even though you ignored him last night. He's in trouble. We're trying to help."

Joel shrugged and returned to whatever spot had kept him totally hidden.

Mom, who was quite used to ignoring the way Joel scared decent human beings, spoke as if my latest heart attack had not occurred.

"What next?" she asked.

"Yeah," Mike chimed in. "What *is* next? We know why Brother Phillip is being blackmailed. We just don't know by who."

"By *whom*," Ralphy corrected. Mike gave him a sour face.

"Slow down, guys," Dad said gently. "Until the fire is proved to be arson, and until it's proved Brother Phillip did it, this blackmail is only speculation."

Dad may have been right, but there was definitely something wrong. It seemed to me that even though Brother Phillip was now physically safe, we still needed to take away the pressure on him. I said that aloud.

Everyone nodded.

I kept thinking aloud. "If we prove nobody is pressuring Brother Phillip, then we have nothing left to worry about. That seems unlikely. If we prove someone is blackmailing him—for the stolen stamps or gambling debts—then we'll know something should be done, and we can go from there."

Dad began pacing the room. "Stephanie has made an appointment for us to visit the street mission's insurance agent this afternoon. Finding out who benefits might confirm or deny our blackmail theory. I think that's the only avenue we have left to explore."

"What about Benito the Bookie?" Mike asked. "We could talk to him."

"Ricky," Dad said, half joking, half not, "make Mike promise not to visit Benito the Bookie. That's a terrible idea."

I looked at Mike. He finally nodded.

I spoke again. "Even without the Benito visit, we might have one more avenue, Dad. And maybe it doesn't lead to blackmail." I didn't like what I was about to say. "We know Brother Phillip was a good kid until college. Then he went crazy for a year. After that, he became a dedicated street preacher for many years. Then, as it appears, he's gone crazy again."

"Are you saying," Mom asked slowly, "that he might have a recurring mental illness?"

I let my silence stand as a "yes."

As they stared at me, I spoke quickly. "Mike, when Imalda and I excused ourselves at the mansion to compliment the cook on his baking, we had a second reason. I wanted to ask him some questions about Brother Phillip, questions that didn't seem appropriate to ask Mr. DuBerg. I didn't find out much more, except one thing. Brother Phillip had been engaged to be married, at least until the stamps were stolen. The cook remembers that day very well, because the girl showed up some time later and heard the bad news from Mr. DuBerg himself."

Mike's eyes widened. "You didn't tell us that in the cab."

"Must have slipped my mind." I grinned to show the opposite, then became serious again. "I also didn't tell you that the cook insisted he had recently seen Brother Phillip driving on a street near the mansion. But the cook was kind of old and crazy, so I didn't know how much of that to believe."

I paused. "But it still wouldn't hurt to find Phillip's ex-fiancée. She might have some answers for us, too." I faced Dad. "May we ask his ex-fiancée some questions while you talk to the insurance people? Bookies and blackmail or not, I can't believe anybody would try a kidnapping or anything like that in the middle of the afternoon."

"I smell some crafty maneuvering." Mom smiled.

"I'd warn you about getting lost," Dad added, "but that smug grin on your face tells me you already have a plan."

I looked at my watch. "Well—"

There was a knock on the door.

"Hellooo," Imalda's voice reached us.

"Now that you mention it, there's our guide," I said. "Right on time."

"Guide?" Mike asked as Mom went to open the door.

Imalda walked in shyly behind Mom. Her dark eyes lit up with a big smile, one I hoped was half special for me.

"Guide," Mike repeated. "Let me guess. We're going to have a girl baby-sit us in New York. Mentioning that slipped your mind in the cab, too, I suppose."

CHAPTER 15

Mike didn't bother hiding his scowl from Imalda as we rode the subway. "Girls," he muttered above the muted clacking of the train. "One smile and they make idiots of *some* of us."

Ralphy ignored him as the four of us stood and swayed to the rocking of the subway train. He was happy to munch from a bag of potato chips and stare wide-eyed at the array of people bumping together in the crowded car. From bums in rags to ladies in furs, from spiked hair to shiny bald to felt hats, they all had one thing in common. Every single person looked straight ahead with blank expressions as they pretended they were alone.

I wanted to pretend I was alone, too. At least away from Mike, whose last comment stamped blushing red across my face.

"Come on, Mike," I mumbled. "She knows the city better than we do."

"So what's wrong with having her brothers along instead?"

"They know she's with us and why." I kept my voice low. "Doesn't that tell you they have confidence in her? Besides, they're on the streets asking more questions about Benito, trying to find out who's behind the kidnapping attempt. I told you that five times already."

"But a girl," he grumbled. "Maybe I should ask her if it's okay to blow my nose?"

She smiled sweetly at him. "What time is it, Mike?"

"Huh?" he blurted. "It's, uh . . ." In the mash of people around us, he fought for room to bend his arm up from the side of his body and twist the top of his wrist toward him.

"Hey! My watch! It's gone!"

I shook my head. "Don't get excited. You probably left it at the hotel room."

"No way. I remember looking at it as we left, because your parents insisted that we return by five this afternoon."

Mike pushed a person jammed beside us as his eyes searched the floor. "Excuse me. I think my watch dropped."

The guy frowned disdain and said nothing.

Mike pushed another person. He covered ten feet ahead and ten feet behind—a struggle that took him three stops of the train and resulted in a steady stream of insults from disgruntled riders.

"Nuts," he said on his return, his voice heavy with disgust. "I can't believe I'd lose a watch so easy."

Imalda offered her first advice since getting on the train with us and enduring Mike's scowls of pride.

"Could be it was stolen," she said.

"Right." Mike's bad mood showed in his sarcasm. "I forgot. You're our guide. You should know how this city works."

He appealed to me. "Come on, Ricky. Tell your friend that watches just aren't stolen right off someone's wrist."

I shrugged. "Big city like this, maybe you were hit by a pickpocket." I grinned and joked to relieve his bad mood. "Still got your wallet?"

"Of cour—" He stopped his sentence just as he slapped the rear of his jeans. "My waalllleettt!" he screamed. "Someone in here stole my wallet!"

His eyes blazed as he searched around the car. Few people glanced our way, part of the elevator habit of pretending nobody else exists besides you.

Mike screamed his frustration. "Give it baaack!" he yelled to no one in particular.

Ralphy thoughtfully crunched on a potato chip, waited briefly to see if anyone would return the wallet, then finished crunching.

Imalda smiled sweetly again. She dug into her waist pouch and pulled out Mike's watch, continuing to smile as she handed it to him. Then she reached in again and placed his wallet in his hand.

"I'm just a dumb girl," she said. "Probably not a good guide or anything like that, but my brothers *have* taught me one or two tricks about city living."

Mike's mouth moved, but no words came out.

"I think," I said, "he's either trying to apologize or ask how you managed to do it."

"If it's an apology, I accept. If it's a question, I can't answer it now. Our stop is coming up."

The train's brakes screeched as it began its rush to a standstill.

I had to prod Mike twice to move him out of his frozen shock.

A man in a yellow-trimmed, full-length blue overcoat—obviously a uniform—opened the doors of the apartment building for us. It was raining lightly, and when we entered, he resumed his hunched stance beneath the canopy outside.

"Fancy," Ralphy whispered again in the hush. "We could play football in a lobby this big."

"May I be of service?" a man asked immediately from behind a polished desk. The yellow-trimmed blue suit perfectly matched the overcoat outside.

"We wish to speak to Jennifer Mitchell," I said, trying to enunciate my words as carefully as his. "But we know which apartment number, so we'll be fine."

Imalda elbowed me. "You don't think places like this have security?"

I felt like kicking myself. The television console in front of the guard made that quite plain.

"I'll ring her," the uniformed man said with a trace of ice in his voice. "We'll let Ms. Mitchell decide what's fine and what's not."

He made no effort to hide the fact that he was looking us over carefully. "What are your names?"

We told him. I also asked him to mention we were here on behalf of Phillip DuBerg.

He lowered his head and spoke quietly into a telephone beside the television monitor. After a few moments he glanced at us with surprise.

A buzzer sounded at a door that separated us from the elevators. "Thirtieth floor," he said. "And no monkey stuff in the elevators. I'll be watching you on camera."

Mike waited less than half a second in the elevator to turn toward Imalda. "I give up," he pleaded. "You win. I'll never doubt you again. Just tell me. How'd you rip me off?"

Imalda winked at him. "Later. That's a promise. I'll show you when we get back to the hotel."

We had no time for more talk. The elevator whooshed to a gentle stop and we filed out. Halfway down the hallway, a woman stood, waiting, with a puzzled smile of greeting.

Imalda gasped and placed her hand on my arm. "It's her," she whispered with awe. "I can't believe it's *the* Jennifer Mitchell."

CHAPTER 16

We must have been close enough for her to overhear the whisper, because we were close enough to see her eyes open with mock horror as she laughed suddenly. "Yes, it's the *real* me," she said through the laugh.

Imalda recoiled. "I'm sorry, I didn't mean . . . it's just that . . ."

Jennifer Mitchell took a step toward us. "I'm the one who should be apologizing. I laughed simply because I don't think it's a big deal to be me. And it always surprises me when other people do. Especially bright-looking young ladies like you."

Imalda responded with a shy smile. "Our family thinks you're the best. You don't make jokes during sad news stories, and you seem to care and—"

Jennifer put a finger to her lips. "Shhh. We should move out of this hallway and into my apartment."

"TV Eleven Six O'Clock Report," Imalda said matter-of-factly as we walked in. "She's the news anchor. You see her face on billboards everywhere."

I nodded but did not speak. I was too busy soaking in the details of the apartment. The large living room—beige leather sofa, large-screen television, low glass tables, CD player—was sunk a half step lower than the rest of the apartment. The dining room, comfortably filled with an eight-chair oak table set, overlooked the city through a full-length window.

Jennifer Mitchell stepped briskly to the kitchen and called back over the open counters, "Hot chocolate? Juice? Diet soda?"

We hung back in a bunch near the entrance.

"Come on, guys," she laughed. "If I don't put a glass into the hands of guests, I feel guilty. Besides, it's a small price to pay for whatever I'm going to find out about . . . about . . . Phillip DuBerg."

"Coke," Mike hollered before her faltered hesitation became strained. "But not diet. That's wimp stuff for . . . for . . ." His voice trailed off as he remembered his watch, wallet, and the simple fact of who was offering him the drink. ". . . girls," he finished weakly.

Imalda kindly ignored him. "Juice."

"Me too," Ralphy and I finished together.

Jennifer leaned over the counter and pointed to the dining room table. "Coats off. Just throw them over a chair. Stop by the kitchen, introduce yourselves. Then have a seat."

She carried a tray with crackers, cheese, and drinks and reached us barely a half minute after we had sat.

In the daylight coming through the dining room window, I had my first clear look at Jennifer Mitchell, anchorwoman for Channel Eleven.

Short, brunette hair, but not cut severe. I tried not to show surprise at the baggy sweatshirt and blue jeans that made her seem so relaxed.

By straining, I remembered that yes, I had seen one or two billboards advertising TV Eleven Six O'Clock Report. But I'm not sure I would have matched the faces without Imalda's reminder.

Both faces were undeniably pretty. Creamy white skin over flawless cheekbones. Straight, delicate nose. Gray-blue eyes.

The face on the billboard had been serious—pencil tucked behind ear—with a slight frown of concentration. The face across the dining room table showed instead tiny and attractive laugh wrinkles at the corners of her eyes.

The face across the table caught my stare and winked at me.

I blushed. "The billboard . . ." I tried explaining.

She moved her lips in distaste. "Part of the news game. I hate the photo they used, but *c'est la vie*. Anything for ratings."

"Well, I'd give you a ten," Mike said stoutly. If, as he accused, a smile from a girl made me an idiot, food from one did the same thing to him.

"Not those kind of ratings," she corrected him with a trace of a smile.

It was Mike's turn to blush.

She let him off the hook by saying two words. "Phillip DuBerg."

Imalda explained how all of us had met Brother Phillip during our first visit.

"Now that you mention it," Jennifer said thoughtfully, "I do recall running a few newsclips about a subway kidnapping gang. All our reporters came back saying some street preacher had declined interviews or publicity. Something about not wanting to create false heroes, he told them. *That* was Phillip DuBerg?"

Her voice had an edge. Excitement maybe? Sad hopefulness? I couldn't tell.

I sipped my orange juice and nodded. "Brother Phillip. Unfortunately, the story doesn't end there." I began to tell her.

"Benito the Bookmaker!" Her eyes narrowed with surprise.

"You've heard of him?" I asked. "This is a smaller town than I thought."

Jennifer studied me intently for a few seconds. I don't know what she was looking for, but she relaxed almost immediately.

"Benito gets around," she said. "Tell me the rest."

I did, including how the cook at the DuBerg mansion had given us her name and address.

"It's been a year since my last letter to Hans," she said fondly, speaking about the cook. "I cried on his shoulder for an hour that terrible afternoon. I'm sure my mascara ruined his apron."

She took a deep breath. "So, you're hoping I might be able to help."

We nodded. Mike's nod, however, didn't slow him for a millisecond on the cheese and crackers.

"First of all, you should know I've done my best to forget about Phillip DuBerg. For the first five years, every single day he crossed my mind. For the last five years..."

She shrugged, then gently took Imalda's hand with both of hers. "Imalda, should you ever be lucky enough to truly love a man, you will know it as certainly as you know each of your hands has five fingers. There are many emotions toward a man that may fool you—infatuation, curiosity, jealousy, anger—into thinking for a while that it is love. But only love gives you a calm and complete certainty. You may or may not be familiar with a New Testament apostle named Paul, but he says it so well. 'Love bears all things, believes all things, hopes all things, endures all things.'"

Jennifer looked up and saw the amazement on our faces, pulled her hands back, placed them in her lap, then spoke softly. "Sorry. I haven't talked about Phillip for so long that today has opened a floodgate."

She probably looked at him every day, I told myself. A framed eight-by-ten photograph of Brother Phillip stood on a two-book stack of hardcovers resting alone on the middle row of a nearby bookshelf. He was much younger but unmistakably recognizable in a white tennis sweater and white shorts, caught in a moment of concentration as he swung his racket at a blurred ball, his free left hand behind him and balancing his body as his right hand followed through.

Jennifer caught my glance. "Yes, I know. Why keep the reminder in plain view if it makes me sad?" She shrugged. "Because I can't not look at it. I'm so sentimental, I even keep it on top of those two textbooks, his. I borrowed them the day that the terrible theft occurred. Anything, I guess, to feel closer to his memory."

Jennifer's face grew softer as she seemed to look inside herself. "The reason I know so much about how true love feels is because that's what I had—have—for that man. Only I didn't discover it until the taillights of his car disappeared, the night I told him to leave."

Then the pain caught up with her. "I can still close my eyes and see those round red lights fading into darkness. By then it was too late to call him back. That's the moment I discovered my love for him could bear all things, believe all things, hope all things, and endure all things. Endure even a two-million dollar theft."

Imalda quietly left the table and returned with Kleenex.

Jennifer dried shiny lines of tears on each cheek and straightened in her chair. "So, what else can I tell you, now that I've made a fool of myself in front of complete strangers?"

Imalda leaned over and dabbed another tear dry for Jennifer. "Not so foolish," she murmured. "We, too, have seen how good a man your Phillip is."

There was a wry smile from Jennifer as she visibly forced strength into herself. "Is, or was? From what you've told me, he's in trouble again."

"Is," I stated as definitely as I could. "That's why we're here. He helped us once and we want to do the same for him. Anything you can tell us about him might help."

I did not want to mention my theory about mental illness; instead, I was hoping she might add some supporting clues without knowing it.

She let her voice become flat and unemotional, a news reporter simply relaying facts. "We met during our second year in college. In the cafeteria. He was reading a book on his tray as he waited in line, and he bumped me. Milk and food everywhere. Then, when I smiled, he dropped his tray completely."

"So romantic," Imalda sighed.

"Pass the cheese," Mike said, his mouth half full of other food.

"He was always reading," Jennifer said. "Anything. Everything. Stayed away from college sports—even though once the halfback of our football team finally got him to agree to a footrace between them. And Phillip won by at least two steps."

Inside, I froze. Outside, I hoped I betrayed nothing. What had

Rocky said about Joel's kidnapper in the parkade? *"Like, I ain't seen nobody move the way that guy did. He's All-Pro if he's anything."*

"About a year later," Jennifer continued, oblivious to my horror, "stories reached me about Phillip and other girls. He told me they weren't true, so I chose to trust him. The stories continued, but he begged me to believe him, not the rumors. Then came the day I showed up at his father's and discovered he'd taken the stamps and run. He returned shortly after and pretended to all of us in the house that nothing had happened. His father told him to leave. It hurt so bad to watch him pack. Him saying nothing. Me saying nothing. I followed him out to the car and we went for a drive. That's when I lost my temper. All the stories and rumors for a year and then the theft that he so coldly ignored. I told him it was finished between us. And he accepted it. Just as coldly as he did the banishment from his father."

Tears started again. "He drove away. And I knew I loved him. Even after all these years have passed. I haven't seen him or heard from him. No matter how much I tried through my network of reporting contacts, I could not find him to deliver the letters that I wrote week in, week out. And I love him just as much today as I did then."

An alarm started chiming from her bedroom.

She answered our puzzled looks, her voice sounding glad to change the subject. "My reminder to start getting ready for work. Sometimes I get caught up in a book and forget the time. I need to leave for the TV station in an hour for the evening news."

We took the hint.

As she opened the door for us, the intercom rang.

"Yes?"

"Ms. Mitchell, you have a visitor." The security guard's voice echoed plainly, yet I didn't recognize it as the person who had rung us through.

Jennifer Mitchell nearly buckled when he continued.

"Should I send him up?" the speaker said. "Calls himself an old friend. Says his name is Phillip DuBerg."

CHAPTER 17

"Impossible," Jennifer whispered.

"Pardon me, Ms. Mitchell?" the intercom voice said.

She was leaning against the wall for support, with her hand still pressed against the intercom button. The security guard could hear her easily.

Without stopping to wonder why my instincts told me it was so important, I waved at Jennifer and put my fore-finger against my lips, pleading her to silence.

She simply stared at me. "Charles," she said tonelessly, "wait one moment."

She released the button and, white as her face was, raised her eyebrows to form the unspoken question.

"Will you see him?" I asked. "Even if this is one of the times—"

"—he's in trouble and won't admit it?" She set her jaw firmly. "I can't *not* see him."

"Then maybe," I said, "it would be a good idea not to mention us." That's what my instincts told me. Whatever state Brother Phillip was in, knowing we suspected a mental illness, or that we doubted him, could not help.

Jennifer gave a short, quick nod.

She pressed the intercom button. "Please send Mr. DuBerg up."

She released the button again. "I'll call you tonight," she said. "This visit can't be a coincidence. Not after ten years."

The four of us were still puffing by the time we reached the main lobby.

"Look at it this way," Ralphy huffed. "We could have had to run *up* thirty floors instead of down."

"Look at it this way," Mike mimicked. "It could be snowing outside instead of drizzling rain." He was still mad that Imalda had beat him down the last flight of stairs.

I understood what he was talking about immediately. There was no place in the lobby for us to hide. Especially with the guard there—glaring at us for having piled through the exit door at a thundering run. And we needed a place to wait—we'd already agreed we were desperate enough for more clues to secretly follow Brother Phillip when he left the apartment.

That meant, as Mike had so sourly noticed, we were forced to go outside into the drizzling rain.

"You're right, Mike," Ralphy said as he lifted his face to feel the cold gray drizzle. "This is better than snow."

Mike shook his head sadly at Ralphy's undiminished optimism and spoke above the traffic noise without real threat. "Good thing, pal, because if it were snow, I'd drift you one."

Imalda tugged on my sleeve. "Across the street. We can slip into one of the doorways."

I made a move to step forward, but she pulled me back. "This is New York. Not Jamesville. You're lucky if drivers stop for traffic lights or cops."

A blur of yellow zipped in front of me. She was right. That taxi probably *wouldn't* have stopped for a jaywalker.

We ran down the street to the corner. We waited until the light had been green for at least five seconds, carefully looked both ways, then dashed across. Imalda led us to a doorway across the street from the apartment lobby, deep enough to keep all four of us pressed out of sight.

"Did you notice the security guard?" I asked to make conversation. "A different one. Probably a shift change. Which is good. He'd have no reason to mention us to Brother Phillip as earlier visitors."

Mike ignored me. He patted his pants to make sure his wallet was still there, then tried an experimental grin at Imalda.

Before he could ask her how she'd picked him so cleanly, the door creaked open from within.

"Whatsa matter? You kids no got no home?"

The old man's grin was friendly enough.

"Sure, but—"

"Inside. This store got everything you need on a day like today."

He waved us in insistently.

I hadn't even noticed we'd chosen the doorway to a small store.

He waved us in again with his gnarled fingers, grinning a near toothless grin under wavy gray hair like steel wool.

Inside, I discovered why we hadn't noticed it was a store. The front window was so tiny, dusty, grimy, and cluttered with army surplus items, it was almost as difficult to see through as a wall.

I ignored the items in the window and concentrated on watching the apartment lobby through a tiny gap as the old man behind us kept speaking.

"You in the store now. You be customers." The old man wheezed an encouraging laugh. "Just like the last one I found in the doorway. Big guy. He's, he's..."

I didn't have to turn around to know the old man's face would be wrinkled into puzzled disappointment. It was obvious in his voice. "Where he be?"

Mike moved beside me and peered outward while whispering from the corner of his mouth. "The guy's crazy. This store's barely bigger than my bedroom. One customer and it's full. If the other guy really was here, we'd know it."

"Hey!" the old man called. "This some kinda game? Now that I think, the other guy, he kept looking straight out the window, too."

A delayed reaction prickled my neck as I realized he had been talking to Mike and me.

"Keep watching," I whispered to Mike.

When I turned around, I saw that Imalda, too, understood the significance of the old man's words. Ralphy, on the other hand, was digging through a pile of rubber boots in a bin in the corner.

"Other guy?" I asked. "How long did he watch?"

"Maybe half hour." The old man flashed his gums in a grin. "But he pay all right. I sold him something every five minutes."

"Do you have a back door?" I asked.

The old man scratched his head. "Think that's where he went?"

I certainly did think. *Who was following us? And why?*

Those two questions repeated themselves again and again over the next fifteen minutes as we waited and endured the running conversation the old man carried.

To keep him happy, Ralphy bought an outdated bottle of water purifying pills and, five minutes later, the goggles of a broken gas mask. The only thing that stopped him from the rubber boots was discovering there wasn't a single matched pair.

And just before he was about to pay another two dollars, this time for an empty cannon shell that the old man assured him was the only one of its kind in North America, Mike hissed.

"Brother Phillip's leaving now. It looks like the doorman is whistling him a cab!"

CHAPTER 18

"Kid"—I received a full-voltage glare and a wash of bad breath as the bulky man in the front seat turned to face me—"this is New York. It ain't a movie."

Imalda smoothly reached into her waist pouch and pulled out a twenty-dollar bill. She folded it lengthwise, waved it in the air near the edge of the front seat, and repeated what I had said, word for word.

"Follow whatever cab that man gets into."

Then she smiled to take away any offense. "This is a bonus above our regular cab fare."

The driver plucked the bill from her fingers without a second thought. "New York, movie. It don't matter that much after all." He peered into his rearview mirror. "Hang on."

Before we could hang on, he gunned his way into a traffic opening, outraced angry horns, barely looked behind him again, then spun a U-turn to put us on the same side of the street as Brother Phillip.

"Not bad," the driver grunted to himself. "I'm not only cute, but a genius behind the wheel."

I sat forward to peer over the cab driver's shoulder and through his rain-streaked windshield. We'd barely made it. Brother Phillip was just now stepping into a cab. Thirty seconds later and he would have escaped.

I didn't even give myself time to worry about the money Imalda had so casually spent. *Time for that later*, I told myself.

In the crowded traffic, it was easy to stay behind Brother Phillip's cab. We spent the last block almost bumper to bumper with it, so when it finally stopped, we had no difficulty seeing where.

"The Carleton 60 Club," Mike read aloud.

"Yup," the cab driver broke his self-enforced silence. "It don't get much fancier. That'll be ten bucks."

I dug in my pocket, then realized something disturbing. "You're not stopping," I told the driver.

"You think I'm stupid, kid? I stop here and that guy'll spot you in a second. We go another half block. And fifty more cents, not including tip. That way, you sneak back and he ain't the wiser."

The cab driver shook his head and muttered into his windshield, "I seen how they do it in movies, too, you know."

We reached the entrance of the restaurant and peered on our tiptoes through the windows in the dark and heavy wooden doors.

There was not much to see. A small speaker's podium, with a man in a tuxedo checking off something in a large book. And, walking away from that podium, Brother Phillip and another man following a waiter.

"Nuts," I said, "too late to see the other guy's face."

We retreated to a nearby alley, sheltered from the drops of rain by an overhang.

"What next?" Mike asked. "We've only got an hour and a half before your parents expect us back at the hotel."

"We need to know who he's with," I answered. "Don't you find it unusual that someone like a street preacher would be meeting someone in a restaurant that fancy?"

Ralphy bobbed his head up and down. "That's what I'd call it, all right. Unusual."

There was silence among us as the rain dripped steadily into the pools of oily water forming in the alley.

"This truly is important, Ricky?" Imalda asked. "Finding out the man he is with?"

I nodded.

She spun on her heels and darted away from us down the alley.

I opened my mouth to speak, but it was too late. She disappeared around a corner.

"Good one, Ricky," Mike said. "At least when girls run away from me it's because I've insulted them."

I raised an eyebrow and peered at him as loftily as I could. "At least," I countered, "I manage to keep my wallet and watch around them."

Mike suddenly took an extreme interest in the toes of his sneakers.

We waited.

A few minutes later Imalda returned, carrying a red vest.

"It's from the restaurant," she explained. "I simply walked into the back and found it in a change room near the kitchen."

"You . . . you can't do that," Mike protested.

"Already did," she said. "And it's not stealing. They'll have the vest back in five minutes."

She held the vest out for Ralphy. "Take off your jacket. Put it on."

"I th-thought you were returning it," he said. It doesn't take much to make him nervous.

"No. I said they'd have it back in five minutes. Not who's returning it. That's *your* job. On your way out again."

His eyes popped wide. "No way. I'm not stupid. 'On your way out again' means I first have to go *in*."

Imalda pulled one sleeve of his jacket away from his arm. "Ralphy," she said patiently, "this is a busboy uniform. Nobody notices busboys. I know; I worked in a restaurant last summer. All you do is go in through the back, walk through the dining room—turning your face so that Brother Phillip doesn't see you if he happens to be looking up—and go to the front of the restaurant. Wait discreetly until the maître d' leaves his reservation book. I promise you he won't notice you, either. Busboys are supposed to stand around waiting for tables to clear, glasses of water to fill. When the maître d' leaves, march to the reservation book as if you own it, then get the name of the man with Phillip DuBerg. On your way out, leave the uniform near the kitchen."

She paused for a breath. "Simple."

"Why me?" Ralph wailed. "I always make mistakes. I'll get caught for sure."

"Why you? You're the only one wearing dark pants. Mike, Ricky, and I have on jeans. No respectable busboy wears a red vest with jeans."

Ralphy appealed to us for help.

Mike and I shook our heads.

"Naturally I'd do it if I could," Mike said, then shrugged.

It took three pushes to get Ralphy going in the right direction.

We waited five minutes under the overhang, saying little. My own nervousness for the scheme was bad enough, I realized; how much worse must Ralphy feel?

Plenty, we discovered at the end of the fifth minute.

He trudged around the corner. Resignation and pasta showed all over his face.

"Don't want to talk about it," he mumbled as he joined us. "Can we go back to the hotel now?"

"Tough day at work?" Mike finally asked.

Ralphy nodded, and two more strands of pasta fell onto the rain-slickened pavement. "I was in a real hurry to get out. I just reached the swinging doors into the kitchen and—"

"—and you went through the wrong door." Imalda shook her head sadly. "I didn't tell him. It's all my fault. In restaurants, everyone's in such a hurry they barge through the doors. They know you go in through the right side and out through the left."

"They don't know it anymore," Ralphy moaned. "Four meals. Four directions."

"Did Brother Phillip notice it was you?" Mike asked.

"Thanks for your concern about *me*," Ralphy said with a trace of bitterness. "I fell face forward. And with food all over me, my mother wouldn't have known who it was."

"Good," I said.

"Good?" Ralphy asked. "Good?"

His voice rose and he stood on his toes to squeak in sudden rage. "Good? You call getting a hundred dollars' worth of pasta and scallops dumped on your head good?"

"Depends on how much got in your mouth," Mike said.

I grabbed Ralphy's fist before he could swing.

"Ralphy," I asked urgently. "The name. Did you get the name?"

"Mr. B. Salingo, and I don't want to talk anymore."

"Salingo!" Imalda shook Ralphy's shoulders. A strand of pasta fell from his hair and stuck to her hand. "Salingo. That's Benito the Bookmaker."

"It's hard to care right now," Ralphy said dully. "I didn't tell you guys the worst part of all."

We watched his mouth curl down in dejection.

"I got fired," he continued in mournful tones. "My first job, and I got fired in less than five minutes. How's that going to look on my résumé?"

CHAPTER 19

Knowing Joel, we should have guessed he was spying. But how can you expect someone in the same hotel room as you to be invisible? Even if it is Joel?

At the time, however, when Joel proved he had been listening, we didn't think it would make a difference. Mom and Dad had left us there to baby-sit him and Rachel while they enjoyed a night out—fancy supper, live theater, all the kinds of things you suspect might be fun, but only when you're a grown-up who needs a slower pace of life.

Imalda had joined us in the hotel room for pizza and videos and discussion of immediate plans to help Brother Phillip, especially after discovering he'd met Benito the Bookie on such good terms at that fancy restaurant.

Rocky, she told us, might be by later if he had more information. Mom and Dad, I'd told her, had talked to the insurance agent. Brother Phillip was not the beneficiary of a fire policy. Instead, it was some guy named Joseph Armwell.

Almost as soon as Imalda had finished that conversation, Mike demanded instructions on pickpocketing.

I coughed. "Pickpockets are not exactly ideal citizens, Mike."

"Hey! I just want to know so it can't happen to me again. Besides, she promised."

I shrugged. Especially since I had an itch of curiosity

myself. A tiny one, of course.

Ralphy, Mike, and I stood in the center of the suite as Imalda explained.

"First of all," she started, "you gotta know the Vasquez family don't do this anymore. It's why—" she closed her eyes and searched for words—"*part* of why we want so bad to help Brother Phillip. This afternoon I had twenty bucks to give the driver. That's because my mama gave me lots, and told me not to worry, as long as we're helping that man."

Imalda paused. "You maybe think we have that gratitude because of how he helped rescue us that last time you were in New York. It's only part. He did more than just rescue us from a kidnapping gang.

"You see, for years the Vasquez Boys—me too—did things you think you have to do on the streets to make it. Like this pickpocket stuff. On the streets, you don't think you need to worry about right or wrong. Just whatever gets you to tomorrow."

Her smile became very shy. "After you guys went back to Jamesville, Brother Phillip took some time with the Vasquez family. He told us how God makes life way more important than just getting to tomorrow."

Her smile grew more confident. "It's hard to explain, but we understood. We saw how it worked in his life. We remembered you guys."

"Us?" Mike asked.

"You guys. I mean, you don't *talk* about being Christians like it's just the *talking* that will convince people. You just *live* like God is part of life. And the Vasquez family finally understood. So we're living that way and ... well, we're not perfect ... but we've got the faith now. All of us."

I started laughing.

Mike elbowed me. "Doughhead. She wasn't telling a joke."

I managed to stop laughing. Then I explained. What had Mom said only this morning? *"And now you want me to trust the three of them to a street gang? . . . What kind of influence will they be on the boys?"*

Imalda joined in our new laughter. Halfway through, she held up a wallet.

Ralphy shrieked.

She held up another wallet.

I shrieked.

Mike grinned a smug smile and pulled his wallet from his front pocket. "I, at least, learned my lesson today."

Ralphy and I groaned.

When the noise died down, she said, "Picked them on the way in. It's easy, once you know the basics. And if you practice."

She walked a tight circle around Mike and accidentally nudged his shoulder with hers. When she faced him again, she held his wallet.

"Shouldn't have returned it to your back pocket," she said.

He grimaced. "What's the secret?"

"Distraction. I bump your shoulder and you feel that instead of what I'm doing to your wallet. In any crowd, someone's always bumping you, so it's easy." She laughed. "I'm not worried about you guys making a living at this. Even if you wanted to, knowing the principle is only half. You got to practice and practice until you can get the wallet with only a touch."

"My watch," Mike said. "No shoulder bump can distract me that much."

"Hold out your arm." She shook her head. "No, dummy, the one with your wristwatch."

Mike did.

She circled her hand around his wrist. A split second later she showed us his watch.

"Hey! That's impossible." Mike's jaw dropped. "I didn't feel a thing."

Imalda disagreed. "Yes, you did. That's how I got away with it. I squeezed the band slightly, enough to add pressure. When the strap releases, your skin feels the impression and still thinks the watch is there, even when I've pulled it away."

"But, but, but—"

"How did I undo the strap?"

Mike nodded.

"Let me guess," I said. "Quick fingers and practice, practice, practice."

She smiled agreement and went on. "Last thing. Some museums or other public places have signs that say 'Beware of Pickpockets.' Maybe sometimes the pickpockets themselves put up those signs."

Ralphy groaned his confusion. "Why?"

She answered with a question. "What's the first thing you do when you see a sign like that?"

"Check for your wallet," Mike said fervently.

"Of course," Imalda said. "Pickpockets love it. It shows 'em exactly where you keep it. Now let's practice."

That's how we spent the next half hour. In practice. Imalda showed us finger techniques so quick and coordinated that we felt like we were wearing mittens as we tried them.

Knowing Joel, we should have known he was spying instead of watching television in my parents' room of the suite.

Our first hint of his presence was as he walked past Ralphy and examined Ralphy's wallet one step later. The little twerp must have heard every word and practiced quietly behind the couch the entire half hour.

"Tell me he's not a natural at this," I moaned. "I get enough grief from him as it is."

Imalda did not have time to answer. The phone rang instead.

"Hello," I said cautiously. Then I waved Ralphy and Mike quiet as I listened. A few minutes later I said yes and hung up.

I didn't even bother trying to tease them with suspense. "That was Jennifer," I told them calmly despite the tremors peppering my stomach. "With no time to say much. She's at the station trying to get together a crew for an emergency news story tomorrow morning."

I stuck out my hand and glared at Joel. He handed me my wallet back.

"She needs us to be part of it," I continued. "Worse, she needs Joel."

"Joel!" Mike and Ralphy echoed.

I felt for the edge of the couch and sat down. "Yeah. He needs to be part of the setup with Benito the Bookie." I swallowed. "They want Joel to carry a knapsack with a hundred grand in cash."

CHAPTER 20

You don't get much sleep the night before a sting operation that involves a television camera crew, $100,000, and a kid brother you can't trust with your wallet. But even after a restless night, you don't feel tired the next morning because every nerve in your body is ready to jump and run away from you in hot cold fear.

It was Saturday morning—only two days after our arrival in New York—and it seemed two weeks had passed. Enough time, as well, for too many questions to haunt me.

I could not shut those questions out as all of us crammed into the minivan taxi that was taking us to meet Jennifer and the camera crew at Hugo's diner.

Who would try to kidnap Joel, and why? And would they try it again?

What about the kidnapper's running speed in the parkade? Was it—as I insisted to myself—a coincidence that Brother Phillip had been equally fast during his college days?

We still knew nothing about Joseph Armwell. Who was he and why did the fire insurance money belong to him?

And finally, what about the good man named Brother Phillip, the man who had done so much for Joel six months earlier, the man who had led the Vasquez family to faith in God? Why had he done such terrible things ten years earlier to drive him from his family and the woman he loved? What was going so terribly wrong for him now to make these strange events swirl around him like the smoke from a smoldering fire?

"Ricky." Mike jabbed a not very gentle poke into the side of my ribs.

"Huh?" I blinked as I came out of my thoughts.

"I asked, twice actually," Mike said, "whether you'll want breakfast at the diner."

"Oh, right. Breakfast." Did he ever think about anything except food? "Only if we have time. Jennifer said she'd explain everything when we got there."

Dad was in the front passenger seat of the taxi. Ralphy, Mike, and I were in the seat at the back, while Joel and Mom shared the middle seat with Rachel in her car seat. It was crammed. Very crammed.

Those had been Jennifer's hurried instructions. Take the entire family to Hugo's diner. Meet her and the crew at nine o'clock sharp. She had promised it would solve all of Brother Phillip's problems.

I hoped it would also answer some or all of my questions.

"It's getting bad," Ralphy commented, "when you get so used to the noise of all this traffic that you think it's normal."

"What noise?" Mike asked.

"Like I said." Ralphy went back to studying the staggering variety of people, buildings, and vehicles that filled our view as our taxi moved down the street.

I sat in silence, making sure my wallet was still in my pants. Whatever Joel had learned by spying on us the night before, he had learned too well. Trouble was, he thought it was a game. Worse, with Joel, the concept of private property had never meant a thing at the best of times, especially when that private property belonged to an older brother. I steeled myself to months of having things taken not only in my absence—as usual—but from my clothing as I was wearing it.

It was almost enough of an injustice for me to stop worrying about what might happen to Joel as he carried the $100,000, or even why Jennifer insisted it be him.

Mom obviously thought the same. It was the first subject she tackled after the introductions had been made in the diner and after Hugo had brought coffee and Danishes for everyone.

"Ms. Mitchell," Mom said, "you have to understand I'm very nervous about your plans for Joel."

"I understand completely," Jennifer replied. "Now that we have a little time, I'll explain everything."

Jennifer swept her arm wide to indicate the table beside us. "As you can see, only two crew members. Rob"—the short, blond man with a pleasant smile nodded—"will be operating the camera and sound system from a nearby van. The other guy, Louis"—a black man with a flattop haircut—"is a bodyguard our station has been using for security over the last three months."

Mom nibbled on her lower lip. Years of experience told me it meant unease. But with her usual patience, she refrained from interrupting Jennifer until everything had been said.

"Our station has been working on a crime exposé series," Jennifer hurried on. "As you may or may not know, here in New York, some of the kingpins are involved in more than one aspect of crime. Benito the Bookmaker, the man we've been trying to expose, is a prime example. Drugs, gambling, loan-sharking, he has his fingers in all of it. We've desperately been trying to prove it. Not only will it guarantee our station massive publicity, but it would put him in jail."

She stirred her coffee without bothering to drink. Her gray-blue eyes glowed with determination. "We've got background on him. We've got witnesses who will speak off the record. We've got police records. We've got suspicions. But we've got no proof. No witnesses who will say anything on camera; they're too scared. No financial records to show crime. No nothing."

She finally sipped her coffee. She looked Mom straight in the eyes. "Until last night."

Jennifer turned to look at me. "Remember you mentioned Benito in my apartment? It startled me, coming out of the blue like that when we'd been chasing him for so long. Then I realized it was a bizarre coincidence. That is, until Phillip stopped by my apartment with his story, and I thought of it instead as a wonderful coincidence."

"Coincidences," my mother said softly. "God's way of working a miracle and remaining anonymous."

Jennifer smiled back. "I'll let Phillip explain everything to you about the blackmail and debt after we nail Benito with solid proof. He mentioned he'd like that privilege. But I can tell you that Phillip and I worked out a way for him to dump his blackmailers and send them to jail at the same time. In short, Phillip will pay them a hundred thousand in cash, and we'll record the transaction on film. There's a microphone hidden in the knapsack. The film, plus getting their conversation on tape, will finally give us the solid proof we need on Benito."

"But Joel?" Mom's voice reflected concern. Joel looked up with a dreamy expression of contentment. He had a piece of pastry on the table in front of him and his teddy bear beside him. It didn't take much to make him happy.

"It was Phillip's idea," Jennifer said. "Benito's too smart a criminal to get trapped. But if he sees Phillip at the meeting place with a small boy nearby, he'll know it's a legitimate transaction, because he knows Phillip would never risk Joel's life. In other words, with Joel around, Benito knows the cops won't try to make a bust."

"Does Benito have a reason to harm Joel?" Dad asked. We were all thinking about yesterday's kidnapping attempt.

Jennifer shook her head. "No reason at all."

"I still don't know," Mom said with hesitation.

"That's why we have Louis." The bodyguard nodded. He wore a loose jacket and pants. Neither article of clothing hid the fact that he rippled with muscle. "Former FBI man. Black belt judo. And if that isn't enough, he's got a .88 handgun in a holster strapped to his ankle beneath his pants. As you can see, he's dressed to be a casual bystander. Even if Benito tries anything—which he won't—Louis will be nearby. And Louis is ready to intercept Benito and the money as soon as he says enough on tape to incriminate himself. We consider it so safe that we're not even worried about the hundred thousand dollars in Joel's knapsack."

"All cash?" Dad asked. "Why actual cash?"

"There's no way Benito will say anything incriminating unless he sees the cash payoff," Jennifer replied. "As I said, Mr. Kidd, our station thinks there's so little risk, it temporarily withdrew the money from our bank. Joel, of course, will be in no danger at all."

At that moment Brother Phillip walked into the diner.

I think it was the gray exhaustion that filled his face that changed Mom's mind.

"Okay," she whispered. "Anything to help that man to a normal life."

Brother Phillip tried a smile as he approached our table. "Good morning, everyone. I hope you're all feeling fine about this. Words cannot tell you what it means for the chance to get back to helping the street people again."

He glanced at Jennifer and then stared deeply in her eyes. "Thank you," he said simply. "You've arranged a miracle."

CHAPTER 21

"Phillip," Hugo commanded from behind the counter.

Brother Phillip spun around immediately. The knapsack filled with $100,000 in cash slapped against his leg. For a split second the fear on his face betrayed his nervousness at the task ahead. Then he found his smile and kept his grip on Joel's hand.

"Yes, Hugo?"

The big man with the apron motioned at a shelf beneath the counter. "Make this another one for my scrapbook."

"Sure, Hugo. I'll do just that."

The door closed behind Brother Phillip and Joel.

That left waiting—among the other diners and Hugo—Mom, Dad, baby Rachel, Mike, Ralphy, Imalda, who had arrived moments before Jennifer and the two-man crew had left, and me.

"Scrapbook?" Mom asked Hugo to ease the tension of silence.

"Yes, ma'am. Last time your sons were in New York, newspapers ran stories for two days. I keep them in a little scrapbook."

Dad nodded. "Must be important, keeping it so close."

"Important, yes. But usually I keep it in a back closet, high out of reach. Not below the counter"—Hugo glanced down—"where too many people can paw through."

He shrugged before anyone could ask the logical question. "Just that Phillip wanted a look through for old time's sake. Haven't put it back yet."

"Wanted to look at it?" I echoed. That seemed strange.

Hugo nodded.

Before I could ask anything else, Ralphy's groan cut through the nervous atmosphere. Jennifer had promised it would be only an hour. With every second feeling like a minute, I didn't dare guess at how long the hour would take.

"The teddy bear." Ralphy pointed. "Joel left his teddy bear."

Mike and I joined in his groan. It was like throwing gasoline on fire, to add to Joel's normal unpredictableness by sending him away without his teddy bear.

"Ricky," Mom said gently, "see if you can hurry up and catch them. I'm sure Jennifer will understand that the last thing she wants is Joel yearning for his teddy bear and wandering back here to find it instead of staying with Brother Phillip."

I nodded.

"I'll go, too," Imalda said. "I know a shortcut to their meeting place. We'll catch them halfway there."

I left with her in such a hurry that I forgot my jacket.

Imalda was wrong. We didn't catch them until they were already in the deserted alley that Benito had chosen for the rendezvous.

I didn't see the surveillance van or Louis, but that didn't surprise me. The meeting wasn't to take place for another forty-five minutes.

We hurried forward, with enough butterflies about the whole operation already to be sneaking as quietly as we could. Although Brother Phillip and Joel were only a good throw to second base away, we didn't call out. That's how much tension we felt.

For once I didn't blame myself for feeling like a chicken.

Worn grime showed air pollution and age on the brick walls of the warehouses that backed into the alley. Litter underfoot forced us to pick our way over the buckled pavement. An eerie quiet muted the city noise and made me shuffle with fear past every darkened doorway.

Brother Phillip and Joel had just reached the place where a garbage Dumpster stood opposite a gap between warehouses. By then we were close enough to let me call out in quiet tones.

"Brother Phillip!" I held out the teddy bear so he would understand immediately.

Once again, as he turned, the flash of tightened skin across cheekbones betrayed his nerves. Instead of the smile he had offered Hugo in the diner, a frown turned down both corners of his mouth.

"This is no place to be," Brother Phillip returned in an equally low voice.

I winced at his brief anger. "I know. It's just that Joel needs this."

To show I didn't want to hang around, I merely tossed the teddy bear across the remaining distance between us. Brother Phillip grunted and caught it in his left hand. With his other hand, he waved us away.

Imalda and I backed up, half trotting as we retraced our steps.

Without warning, a mountain of muscle stepped from a doorway and blocked us so quickly that I nearly fell as I stopped!

Before I could squeak out any surprise, a huge hand clapped itself on my shoulder.

Louis the bodyguard. I sagged with relief.

"You scared me to—"

"Turn around." He cut me off.

Imalda was already looking behind us.

I shivered, and not because it was a November morning and I wore only a T-shirt and jeans.

Back at the Dumpster, Brother Phillip was speaking to a man in a dark suit. The knapsack of money was on the ground between them. Joel stood a step away at the side. But what sent my blood backward in my veins was the fourth person there—the short man holding three Doberman pinschers, each straining its leash to a tight, quivering strand of leather.

Louis dropped his hand from my shoulder abruptly and walked toward them.

They spotted him almost immediately.

The man in the dark suit held up his hand, apparently a signal to hold the dogs in place.

"What's with the dogs?" Louis said, his voice carrying clearly. "It's like pointing a loaded gun. I don't like this."

"Too bad," the man with the dark suit said. "Don't move any closer."

"That's not how it's going to work," Louis said. "I don't want the kid in any danger."

I knew I was terrified. Every cell in my body told me that. But my brain somehow ignored all the safety signals and forced my feet to follow Louis.

The man in the dark suit smiled. And leaned forward to unsnap the chains that held the dogs by the collars.

"The kid!" Louis shouted at Brother Phillip. "Give them the money and save the kid!"

Instead of turning and crouching to protect Joel, Brother Phillip reached down for the knapsack, hefted it in his left hand, and bolted around the dogs!

I could not believe what my eyes plainly told me. Brother Phillip melted away the distance between us, and before I could pound out another three steps, he had disappeared around a far corner.

By then Louis was nearly to Joel. Imalda and I were only steps behind.

The man in the dark suit moved to safety behind his short partner, leaving the now unchained dogs as a menacing wall between them and Louis.

"Benito the Bookie," Louis said with breath-shortened words. "The money's gone. It's Phillip you want. Not the kid."

"No chance." The man in the dark suit spoke with no emotion. His eyes were black, staring out from deep sockets. The skin around his mouth barely moved as he pushed each word clearly between razor-thin lips. "We take the kid. He's leverage for us to get the money back. Make a move and my friend here will say a single word, and the dogs will rip the kid to shreds." Benito's voice had the authority of evil.

I was still reeling over Brother Phillip's actions. He'd taken the money! Left Joel in danger! Now, through the shock, an anger and fear for Joel's safety clutched at me.

Louis had no choice but to remain frozen in place.

"Glad you see it my way," Benito's voice caressed. "I take the kid. My friend here stays. You so much as twitch, he gives the command for all three dogs to attack. Five minutes from now you and the other two kids back away very, very slowly. When you've reached the end of the alley and have gone from sight, my friend takes his dogs away. And you don't follow. Understand? Now let go of the kid. The dogs won't touch him."

The short man whispered something to his dogs. They parted as Benito stepped between them and yanked on Joel's arm.

Benito didn't even look back as he walked in the direction Brother Phillip had fled. He left behind him the short man with three angry dogs, still facing Louis across a small gap of no-man's-land.

And, fallen on its side between the dogs and Louis, Joel's abandoned teddy bear remained in silent protest.

CHAPTER 22

When I become a parent, I hope I remember how you never know when a small moment will arrive to make a big impression on your kid.

For me, it was the way Mom answered the knock on the door of our hotel suite Sunday at noon, over a full day after Joel had been kidnapped.

Early Sunday had been spent in a nearby church. Prayer never seemed more appropriate. Joel—and Benito the Bookie—had vanished. The police had been sympathetic but didn't seem hopeful. "A big city," one barrel-chested cop had told us. "We'll do our best, but it's a big city. And Benito knows every hidden nook and cranny."

Words of little comfort.

When that knock interrupted our gloominess half an hour after returning from the church service, none of us expected to see Jennifer Mitchell.

She walked in slowly past Mom and then waited, standing with bowed shoulders and her hands clasped in front of her. Her clear gray-blue eyes were reddened with fatigue. Her hair was unbrushed. She did not start to remove her coat.

In that simple, small moment, Mom closed the door with a quiet click and placed a comforting hand on Jennifer's shoulder. In that simple, small moment, I suddenly realized how much dignity and care for other people my mom carried inside her.

Jennifer was the woman who had pledged—wrongly—safety for Joel. Yet Mom was the woman giving comfort, not asking for it, nor did Mom condemn Jennifer for the sudden loss of her son.

I think Jennifer understood the comfort being offered. She blinked back tears and smiled. "I had to come here," she said. "I've had no sleep. Your son is gone. And I'm going crazy with worry and guilt."

Jennifer rubbed her eyes. "You seem so calm. How do you do it?"

Mom led her to a chair. "We're as worried as you are. But there comes a time when you've done everything humanly possible in a situation and all that's left is trust in God." Mom paused. "We're there."

Mom moved to sit on the sofa beside Dad and me. Mike and Ralphy sat glumly opposite us, leaning against the wall and hugging their knees to stare at no place in particular.

"Don't put the blame on yourself," Dad told Jennifer. "We, too, trusted Brother Phillip."

At that statement, everything overwhelmed me again. The anger, the confusion, the fear, the shock. *What had gone so terribly wrong to make Brother Phillip take the money and leave Joel? How could that man betray us so badly?*

I found myself pacing the room.

"Ricky," Mom said in a low voice, "we've already discussed all of this. Don't let it hurt you again and again."

I let out a deep breath. "What happened, Ms. Mitchell? How could he have done that to all of us? Joel would have been totally safe if he hadn't done that. Taking the money, everything. He used us and ran away."

"I've tortured myself with the same questions. That's why I'm here. Looking for answers."

Jennifer sat forward and placed her hands in her lap. "When you guys left me on Friday afternoon"—she opened her hands in a wave that included Mike, Ralphy, and me—"the thought of seeing Phillip again after ten years of regret and love without him made me so weak I could barely stand. And when he walked through the door, it was all I could do to keep from throwing myself into his arms."

Jennifer blushed. "We kissed."

She recovered and gazed at the floor. "It wasn't the same. In that single second I discovered I had been fooling myself for ten years. I had only imagined the love. To see him in person, to feel him hug me, was not what I dreamed it would be."

Mom put a hand on her shoulder again.

Jennifer patted it. "Oh, I'm fine about that. It was a relief, actually, to be free of an impossible love after all that time."

She resumed the straight-backed posture of a reporter relating a factual story. "It was the same for Phillip. At least, he *seemed* businesslike about everything. He told me the story about Benito that he was going to tell you. One day Benito calmly approached him and demanded blackmail money. Otherwise, Phillip told me, the bookie would tell everyone about Phillip's past and the two-million-dollar theft. Phillip was desperate enough to take a chance with some of the mission's money. He had an inside tip on a horse race, and he hoped a good gamble would be enough to come up with the money Benito demanded."

A soft, ironic laugh came from Jennifer as she stopped to find her next words. "Instead, Phillip unknowingly placed the bet with the same bookie who had been blackmailing him. He lost. And lost again trying to make up for the first loss. Before he knew it, he was a hundred thousand dollars in debt."

"But the fire," Mike asked. "Did Brother Phillip start that?"

"He promised he hadn't. But after yesterday..." Jennifer's shrug told more than anything she could have said.

My brain hurt so badly from confusion that I could feel grooves from the same thoughts over and over again.

"Nothing," I asked, "ever gave you an indication of why he might steal the stamps?"

Jennifer shook her head. "I've thought that through a million times. I've played our good-bye in my mind just as many times. How he didn't fight it when I told him it was over. How he flinched when I threw our engagement ring into the pond."

She sighed. "'The end of the circle' he called it then. Just smiled sadly as the splash reached us, and called it the end of a perfect circle of love."

I spun on her so fiercely that she gasped.

"What did you say?"

"Ricky," Mom said in her no-nonsense tone. "Mind your manners."

"Please," I begged. "What did you say? About the circle."

Jennifer's puzzled frown did not stop her from replying. "Phillip was always romantic. He said that our love had no beginning and no end. Just like a perfect circle. So when I lost my temper and threw the ring into the water, he called it the end of the circle."

I forced myself to breathe normally. Somehow Jennifer had said something significant, but I could not decide what.

I explained what I had heard on the phone but had kept to myself—"*Meet . . . me . . . at . . . the . . . end . . . of . . . circle.*"

"Strange you should think our good-bye might mean something," Jennifer said with hesitation.

We waited.

"When Phillip stopped by my apartment on Friday, he quizzed me again and again about that last afternoon and our time at the pond on the edge of his father's property. It didn't make sense. Finally he left that alone and pleaded for my help on the sting operation."

"Would you have tried to help him even if it didn't fit in with the exposé you'd been working on for three months?" Dad asked.

"I don't know," Jennifer said slowly. "It was the perfect solution for both of us, but even as I agreed to run the idea past the station manager, I knew I would no longer love Phillip. So . . ."

We did not interrupt her painful silence.

After too many moments, she stood.

"Well," she said. "I've taken a great deal of your time already."

She stopped midway through buttoning her coat. "Oh, I nearly forgot."

Jennifer dug into her purse. "Joel's wallet," she explained gravely. "It was in the back of his pants and nearly falling out, so Louis grabbed it just before, just before . . ."

I took the offered wallet.

Mom quickly moved to Jennifer and hugged her. "Don't torture yourself. We'll call you as soon as we hear anything."

In the near vacuum following Jennifer's departure, Ralphy spoke in an odd voice.

"This sounds stupid," he said. "But I never knew Joel had a wallet."

I could not help myself. I pictured Joel's smiling little face and the pleasure he had taken in fooling us by picking our wallets all that morning before being kidnapped, and a tear rolled down my cheek.

"He didn't," I told Ralphy as I rubbed my face dry with my shoulder. "It's one of ours. We just haven't noticed yet because of all our worry."

Absently, I flipped it open. Then stared. It was not a familiar wallet.

I pulled out the driver's license to see Brother Phillip's bearded face.

Two words burned an image in my eyes.

I blinked and read them again. Carefully. The same two words jumped at me. Two words I didn't want to believe.

"Remember how we had decided that since Brother Phillip wasn't the named beneficiary of the insurance policy, it meant he wouldn't have been the arsonist?" I asked with bitterness that verged on hatred.

All of them nodded.

"Wrong," I continued. "If we ever needed proof that Brother Phillip set fire to the mission, we have it now."

I held out the driver's license. "False identification," I

announced. "It's probably all he needed to get the money without suspicion."

"The name the insurance agent gave us," Dad said through tight lips. *"Joseph Armwell."*

Whatever hope and faith I had managed to keep in Brother Phillip as a hero dissolved completely as I heard those two words confirmed aloud.

CHAPTER 23

Hunches are made from the things you see without knowing you see them.

I read that somewhere and never understood it until too much of Sunday night had passed with me standing in front of the hotel window, staring at the lights of the city.

"Give it a rest, pal," Mike mumbled for the tenth time from his bed. "Get some sleep."

I couldn't help smiling. Obviously his own sleep wasn't perfect. The smile left quickly. We both had the same reason for needing a good lullaby. Worry for Joel and anger at Brother Phillip's betrayal filled too much of my mind.

I said nothing and waited for Mike's snores to return.

I stared out the window longer, hoping the thoughts that teased my mind would form into something solid enough to grasp and pull and—

My lungs lurched to a stop as pictures tumbled into place.

Hunches are made from the things you see without knowing you see them.

I forced myself to take a breath and replayed each picture. *Jennifer—sighing at a photograph on a bookshelf of the man she had once loved, a man swinging a racket in his right hand. Hugo—pointing at a scrapbook beneath his counter. Brother Phillip—catching Joel's teddy bear in that lonely alley and, shortly after, grabbing the knapsack with money.*

I played them all, over and over again. Then added them to the wallet that Joel had taken with an ID that didn't belong to Brother Phillip. Not everything fit, but the new equation summed up differently enough to tell me what to do next.

The clock beside my bed glowed 4:03 A.M. in block numbers.

I slipped from the hotel room.

Monday morning.

Breakfast, like every meal since the kidnapping of Joel, was a silent picking at food.

After, we went nowhere but the hotel suite. What was there to enjoy in the city with worry and fear filling all of us? Our flight was booked to return in the evening. School, after all, began the next day, and none of us had planned on losing Joel again in New York. Mom and Dad, of course, would not leave without him. They sat calmly in one corner, holding hands lightly and occasionally murmuring comfort to each other.

It was everything I could do to keep Mike from flipping from the sports channel as we sat and waited for any scrap of information on Joel. I didn't want any of us to have false hope.

"Come on," Mike said. "A city like this has dozens of channels. Let's at least check them out."

"If we don't watch this," I said, "Ralphy will find a science show."

Mike grunted sudden agreement. We stayed with the football game.

None of us really watched it, though. The big questions blocked our concentration every moment. *Where is Joel? Is he still fine?*

I'd been half expecting the phone call, but I still jumped with jangled nerves when it came an hour later.

Dad answered immediately, and his face darkened in thought as he listened. When he hung up, his eyebrows formed slashes of intensity.

"That was Mr. Henry DuBerg," Dad said in a tight voice. "He hoped it would be convenient that a limousine is on its way. He asked if all of us could be ready, including your friend named Imalda."

I nodded. She'd left a number for emergencies or if we needed more help from her brothers.

"I don't understand," Mom said. "Henry DuBerg? That's Phillip's father."

"Yes. He wants us at his mansion."

Mom has always been a mind reader. "Someone's been hurt," she said sharply. "Is it Joel?"

"No, not Joel." But there was an uncertainty in his voice that chilled me.

"Sam! What did that man tell you?"

"They've found Brother Phillip," he said. He let out a breath heavy with sadness. "However, he rolled his car trying to escape the police. Mr. DuBerg told me his son was taken away in a coma. Paramedics at the scene refused to guess if he might live or not."

Mom moved forward and took Dad's hand with both of hers. "And Joel?" she asked.

Dad closed his eyes briefly and shook his head.

"Nothing. Not a sign."

CHAPTER 24

The butler, stiff and proper, made the introductions in the library of the mansion, then departed.

The huge, quiet room seemed to swallow all of us. Jennifer Mitchell was there, standing alongside the chair that held a visibly strained Mr. DuBerg. Mike, Ralphy, Mom, Dad, Imalda, and I faced them across the plush carpet. Joan DuBerg, the butler had explained as he led us down the hallway, had returned to her own residence the day before.

Joel's absence in this group stabbed me with pain.

"I apologize for not standing," Mr. DuBerg began. "This morning's events have taken their toll and reminded me that indeed I am an old man."

He held out his hand in my direction. "Despite sorrow at the accident that involved my son, I want to congratulate you, young man. Your idea was sound, and if the doctors can bring Phillip to consciousness, he will be able to tell us where to find your brother."

Embarrassed, I stepped forward to shake his hand quickly, then stood back again.

"Idea?" Dad asked Mr. DuBerg. "We know little more than what you told me over the telephone. What do you mean, sir?"

"A late-breaking news scoop," Jennifer explained. Her face, too, reflected pain. "I'm surprised Ricky didn't let you know."

"I'm not," Mom said with a trace of ice. "He's been known to do things without asking beforehand."

My face must have told its own story, because after several moments Mom's expression became softer. "Tell us, son."

"First of all," I said, "the reason I didn't say anything earlier was because I was afraid of getting your hopes up for nothing."

"The news scoop," Mike broke in impatiently.

"I called Jennifer from the hotel lobby while you were sleeping. I simply asked if she would risk planting a false news story."

"At a quarter after four in the morning," she added. "While no sane person is capable of logical thought, I made a difficult ethics decision."

Dad raised his eyebrows in question.

"Was it worth deceiving the public to try saving a six-year-old boy?" she answered. "I didn't take long to decide."

"The news scoop," Mike urged.

I made a mental note to make sure Mike had food around him as often as possible. It was the only way to keep him quiet.

"Jennifer promised to use her connections to broadcast the solving of a crime," I answered him instead of speaking my thoughts. "All the television and radio stations in the area began reporting a vague story that new facts on the ten-year-old theft of two million dollars in stamps had led to the case being reopened by the police."

"I think I want to sit down," Ralphy said flatly. "This is getting to be too much for me."

"That's what I thought at first," Jennifer said. "Then Ricky explained why it was so urgent. And I understood why he called me so early."

Once again attention focused on me.

"She needed to get the story out as soon as possible," I said. "I didn't know if four in the morning was giving enough notice."

"Why?" Imalda asked. "What could that news story do?"

"Sir," I said to Mr. DuBerg, "we haven't even had a chance to ask you about the police chase. It did begin nearby?"

He nodded.

"From the road that led to the pond," Jennifer confirmed. "Just like you guessed."

"It fits, then. I'll try to answer the why," I said. "The fact that the police did spot him there means I was at least partly right."

I searched for the way to begin. "Jennifer told us yesterday that Brother Phillip had seemed too businesslike and had spent a lot of time asking about their final good-bye on the day the stamps had been stolen. I wondered why that would be so important to him, when he already had enough problems with his $100,000 debt and the burning of the street mission. The only thing that made sense was the missing stamps. And, I decided, if he wanted to know where they were—after all this time—it meant he didn't have them."

Dad held up his hand. He spoke slowly and thoughtfully. "And if he didn't have them, why ask Jennifer? Unless he suspected she knew something he didn't."

I nodded. "I thought the stamps might make the perfect bait. If Jennifer could bluff him into thinking he had a chance of getting them first, he might fall into the trap. But she had to get the news out quickly, just in case Brother Phillip was about to leave town. Because, of course, there would be no way for her to spread the story beyond her New York connections."

Jennifer smiled sadly. "Ricky predicted that it would not take much for Brother Phillip to return to the scene of our final farewell."

I smiled just as sadly in return. "It's like the way a guilty conscience works. I just said I thought it wouldn't take much of a news story to get him searching there again."

"Thirty seconds," Jennifer explained. "The story only took thirty seconds of air time. We gave a background on the theft and then said new facts as relayed by someone close to the family had given police cause to reopen the case. Phillip would know that the someone close to the family was me and draw his own conclusions."

Mr. DuBerg spoke from the chair. "Phillip must have decided to take one final search of the one place he always suspected the stamps might be. Because that's where the hidden police spotted him.

Driving to that pond on the far edge of our property. When they sounded the siren, he tried escaping. His car left the road at a turn near the river and . . ."

Mom and Jennifer both moved closer to the old man.

"Sir," I said quietly. "On your property, I've seen small buildings. May I presume there is one near the pond?"

Jennifer spoke quickly to spare Mr. DuBerg. "Yes."

My voice remained serious and quiet and I did not look away from him. "I pray within an hour you will have your son back. The way you remember him."

He looked past the tears brimming his eyes. "Please, don't mock an old man."

Mom shot me a thunderous warning glance.

"It's okay, Mom. Really." Suddenly the fatigue of carrying the rest of my guesses in worried silence hit me in a numbing wave. I wanted to sob with relief. The relief of being able to tell everything. And the relief of love for Brother Phillip and Joel.

Instead, I clenched my fists to hold the emotion.

"I think they're out near the pond," I said. "Brother Phillip. And, I hope, Joel."

They stared at me as if I were crazy.

Maybe I was. But no other explanation fit everything that had happened.

"But before we go look," I finished, "I think it would be smart to take along as many of your security guards as possible."

CHAPTER 25

"It's a guest cottage, actually," Jennifer explained without having to raise her voice above the tranquility around us. "As you can see, this property has acres and acres of land, and when Henry DuBerg the First established his fortune, he scattered several of them out of sight of the mansion."

If the situation were not so serious, I might have laughed at the appearance all of us presented as we formed a convoy of electric golf carts—vehicles Henry DuBerg the Third had informed us were a routine method of transportation on the property.

It didn't surprise me. The property itself could have been a well-manicured golf course. The gray November skies of the previous few days had relented. In the sunshine and warming air, and with the view of the rolling hills leading down to the Hudson River, the ride should have been glorious.

Instead, it filled me with fear.

What if I had guessed wrong? Five golf carts, filled with security guards and my friends and family, all here because I had promised them two people special to all of us.

We reached the rise of a small hill, and as we began to dip downward, I saw the guest cottage. It fronted a medium-sized pond, and a narrow paved road led away from it.

"The place of our last good-bye," Jennifer said.

The end of the circle. I hoped.

"You're sure," I asked for the fifth time, "that the man the police caught never got as far as the cottage before turning around and driving away?"

"Very sure." She smiled, and I nearly blushed at how good the sun looked dancing off her gray-blue eyes. "For the fifth time, I'm very sure."

That, indeed, was a consolation. It meant that our convoy might be a total surprise to whoever was inside the cottage.

Going down the hill—third in that slow-moving line of golf carts, with Ralphy and Mike beside me on the padded seat—became one of those moments where you want the events to happen quickly and end the suspense, but at the same time you want the suspense to last forever because you're afraid of the results.

So I did the only thing you can do during a moment like that. I closed my eyes and prayed briefly. Not to ask for a miracle, but to tell God I was scared and that I knew He was in control. At least that's the way it began, but I couldn't help but end by asking for as much help as possible from Him. If Joel and Phillip were in there but not alone, the worst could happen. Because I had a terrible suspicion about who was there with them.

Too soon, we were there.

It was a tiny cottage, barely larger than a car garage. White wood siding. Green-shingled roof. And a sliding glass door leading to a deck that faced the pond.

Some of my fear dissolved as Mr. DuBerg, in the lead cart, firmly barked out his orders. His grief well hidden, he was doing what his background had trained him to do—make decisions and give instructions.

"Fan out. Surround the cottage."

Within seconds all ten of the men in security uniforms had done just that.

I caught a movement in one of the shuttered windows. I braced myself for the worst.

"The rest of you, move well back, and keep the carts between you and the cottage," Mr. DuBerg continued. The need for his leadership had added strength to his actions.

We began moving back. Dad, however, marched to Mr. DuBerg's side.

"I, too, may have a son in there," Dad said clearly enough for us to overhear.

Mr. DuBerg simply nodded. Both of them waited.

Then Mr. DuBerg spoke.

"If you look out your windows," he called loudly. "You will see a small force of men trained to deal with any situation. Furthermore, the police are on their way and shall arrive within ten minutes."

More waiting.

Then a voice snarled from within. "We've got two hostages. Expensive hostages."

Benito the Bookie! I was right!

Then I sobered. Being right didn't mean this was over.

"Does this mean you wish to negotiate?" Mr. DuBerg asked.

"Of course, you uppity rich snob. We deal. In the next five minutes. Or else."

Mr. DuBerg remained unperturbed and made an instant decision. "All of us will retreat to the top of the rise east of here. That gives you five hundred yards. Enough distance for you to escape before the police arrive. Close enough for us to see that you've left the hostages behind."

The quick reply to that statement hinted at desperation. "That's a deal," a muffled shout said. "So move now before we change our minds."

Mr. DuBerg nodded and his men reacted with superb precision. The rest of us were bolting for the golf carts. Within a few heartbeats, all the carts were speeding across the grass, and before another minute had passed, we were at the top of the rise.

Mr. DuBerg snorted disgust. "Those fools! They'll never get

past the security system on the outside walls."

Three men—one of them Benito the Bookie—scurried from the cottage, barely stopping to notice our position. They disappeared at a full run into the trees on the far side of the pond.

Then, slowly, two more figures moved onto the deck of the cottage. One, tall and stooped. The other, short and reaching up to hold the man's hand.

Even from this far away, I was ready to say that I could see them blinking in the sunlight. But then, I've always had an imagination that worked overtime.

CHAPTER  26

"Three things," I said around a mouthful of pink salmon. "Three things gave it away."

Quiet clattering of busy knives and forks punctuated the air as I swallowed. The dining room table in Jennifer's condo apartment held a large crowd of us. All happy.

Jennifer sat at the end nearest the kitchen. A celebration supper had been her idea. Henry DuBerg had insisted on paying the ticket difference to reschedule our early evening flights out of New York. It hadn't taken too much convincing to agree. After all, we had Joel back. And the real Phillip DuBerg.

He sat at the other end of the table, with dreamy contentment all across his face. The kind of look that Mike saved for food. Only for Brother Phillip, the reason was Jennifer. She kept beaming the same look in return.

Imalda, sitting on my left, had sized up that situation and whispered a phrase in my ear to describe the staring back and forth between them as a crossfire of love. I had asked her not to spoil my appetite, only because that's what cool guys say.

Joel sat on my right. Mom, with Rachel in her lap, Dad, Ralphy, Mike, and Mr. DuBerg filled the other seats. Hugo and Imalda's brothers had not been able to make it.

Jennifer had left the dining room blinds open, and the

lights twinkling up from the city night made for a background that matched the gourmet supper perfectly.

Following the rescue of Brother Phillip and Joel, there had been too much confusion for all of us to be together. So I had saved whatever explanation I could offer until this supper. I was hoping Brother Phillip would fill in the blanks.

The polite clattering continued as I told them about hunches being made from the things you see without knowing you've seen them.

"The key," I continued after setting down my fork on a completely empty plate, "was discovering the wallet that Joel had taken in fun. It finally occurred to me to wonder if the man he had taken it from was actually someone besides the *real* Brother Phillip."

I nodded at Mr. DuBerg. "When we first visited, you had mentioned that until the stamps were stolen, you had loved Phillip as deeply as any man could love his own son. Phillip was not really your flesh-and-blood son—you had adopted him."

Mr. DuBerg cleared his throat. "Yes, as I mentioned before, it was always something we meant to tell him, but we kept delaying it because, except for the fact that he had not physically been born to us, he truly was our son."

I nodded again and spoke to the rest of the table. Most were finished. Mike, however, was attacking his third helping.

"Remember when Brother Phillip—" I paused and grinned at Brother Phillip at the end of the table—"I mean the *fake* Brother Phillip first visited our hotel suite? How he seemed hesitant? It made sense at the time. He'd just been through a difficult time. Or so we thought. But remember Hugo and the scrapbook at the diner? Why had the fake Brother Phillip asked to look at the newspaper clippings? One answer that made sense was because he needed to know what we looked like so he wouldn't call us by the wrong names."

"The third thing," I said as I stood and moved to the bookshelf on the far side of the table, "was this photograph."

I took it from its resting place atop Phillip's old textbooks and brought it back to the table. The younger version of Brother Phillip in his tennis whites stared back at us from the picture frame.

"The real Brother Phillip is swinging a tennis racket with his right hand. In the alley, when I tossed the teddy bear to the fake Brother Phillip, he caught it with his left hand. And when he grabbed the knapsack and ran, he grabbed the knapsack with his left hand."

I paused for breath. Jennifer reached for the photograph and placed it beside her on the table.

"So," I finished, "finding the wallet with identification that showed Brother Phillip's face but had the name 'Joseph Armwell' finally got me to consider the impossible. Maybe, just maybe, the man who had visited us actually *was* Joseph Armwell, not Brother Phillip. Since Brother Phillip had been adopted, what if he had an unknown twin brother? One posing as Brother Phillip?"

Brother Phillip smiled at me. A different smile than the one he'd been sending in Jennifer's direction since the beginning of the meal, but still a wonderful smile belonging to the man we remembered from our first trip to New York.

"Unknown is right," Brother Phillip said with feeling. "I can still feel the electric shock that hit me when he first walked up to me at college. It was like looking into a mirror."

Joel squirmed beside me. I grabbed his teddy bear and put it in a stranglehold beneath the table. Joel wouldn't dare disappear now.

"I made the mistake of telling him I'd never known I was adopted," Brother Phillip said. "That's when his blackmail—the real blackmail—first began."

Joel tugged for the teddy bear. I kept a firm grip. Everyone else's attention was firmly fixed on Brother Phillip.

"You see," he continued, "Joseph and I had been placed into an adoption agency when we were babies. When Joseph grew older, he managed to find out about his past. That's when he discovered me, and that I belonged to the family I did. It made him bitter, thinking he had not become a DuBerg. So he looked for a way to take advantage of being my twin."

Brother Phillip closed his eyes. The pitch of his voice changed as he remembered the difficult times. "Joseph Armwell lied to me that first day—as he gloated to me again and again during my imprisonment in the cottage over the last few months. This was his lie. He told me that my mother—Henry's wife—had given us both up for adoption a year before becoming Mrs. DuBerg. That she'd been unmarried and didn't want Mr. DuBurg to know about that scandal. Then, after her marriage, she had tried to readopt her true sons."

Mr. DuBerg's face showed regret as he listened. "I'm so sorry, son," he said. "If we would have only told you sooner, you would have been spared the last ten years."

Brother Phillip opened his eyes and shook his head. "God did mysterious things with both of our lives. It led me to becoming a street preacher. Don't blame yourself."

Mike, subtle as always, blurted out, "But how did Joseph Armwell blackmail you back then?"

"Simple," Brother Phillip answered. "He threatened to tell Henry DuBerg that the woman he had married had given birth to us under scandalous conditions, that he had married her without knowing the secret of her previous children."

Brother Phillip looked across at Mr. DuBerg. "It's not important to me that I discover my biological mother now. Your wife was and always will be my true mother. That's why I couldn't let her be blackmailed."

"So," Mr. DuBerg said with a tone of marvel, "you took the blame for everything Joseph Armwell did. Just to make sure this false dark secret of blackmail would never come to light."

"Yes, Father," Brother Phillip said. "I was only twenty. I loved you as fiercely as I loved her. I did not want anything to happen that would destroy your marriage to each other."

Jennifer pursed her lips. "Those stories about other girls."

Brother Phillip nodded. "As long as Joseph was careful, he could live my life. He rubbed it in my face, asking other girls at the college out for dates, and doing some of the other things he did, knowing I would get blamed. He knew I would never reveal to anyone that he existed as my twin brother. It killed me, having people think such bad things about me. And then there was the day he went too far."

"The stamp collection," I guessed. "He showed up during the day. Took the stamps. Hid them when Mr. DuBerg returned early. You appeared that night, not even knowing they'd been stolen."

"Yes. I guessed soon enough who had taken them. And when Father banished me, I knew it was the perfect solution. As long as I was not part of the DuBerg family, Joseph Armwell would not be able to pose as me and threaten them. So I ran away, intending to be gone forever."

He paused. "I attended Mother's funeral, but even then I was disguised."

My mom sighed. "You said good-bye to everything you loved. And you knew everyone you loved thought the worst of you."

"It was more than just protecting my mother's name. It was keeping her from losing Father. Or keeping Father from losing her. I thought if I stayed, the three of us would be hurt. If I left, only one of us would be. Me." Brother Phillip's light grin did not hide the pain in his eyes. "And I was too young to see any other way."

CHAPTER 27

The conversation shifted back and forth, continuing well into the round of cheesecake with whipped cream that Jennifer served for dessert.

Brother Phillip explained all of what had happened when Joseph Armwell finally found him ten years later.

It had been a terrible fluke. One of Benito the Bookie's men had met Joseph in an upstate prison. Joseph had been there for check forgery. Benito's thug had jumped with surprise to see the man he thought of as Brother Phillip the street preacher. Over time they got to know each other. Once, in passing, Joseph had mentioned Brother Phillip's connection to Jennifer Mitchell, the TV Eleven news anchor. When that got back to Benito, he made a proposal to Joseph.

Would Joseph, Benito had asked, be interested in sharing some fire insurance money? Benito agreed to supply the muscle. Joseph agreed to supply the actor—himself—as soon as his prison term ended.

As soon as Joseph was free, they kidnapped Brother Phillip. Joseph, from his early days of posing as Phillip DuBerg, knew about the rarely visited guest cottage, and had reasons unknown to Benito for suggesting it as the perfect hostage place.

Benito had actually suggested killing Brother Phillip,

but Joseph, with his secret reasons, had stopped that idea. And Benito had his own secret reasons for keeping Joseph happy—he was waiting for a way to get at Jennifer Mitchell through Joseph.

Joseph began his life as a fake Brother Phillip. He and Benito began to circulate the story that Brother Phillip had a terrible debt, preparing for the day Joseph could burn down the street mission. They both knew that had Brother Phillip been the insurance beneficiary, arson would be suspected. But, with proof that he was Joseph Armwell, he planned on having little difficulty collecting the insurance money under that name. Especially because they made sure to pick an insurance agency with people who had never seen Brother Phillip as Brother Phillip. Nobody, they knew, would make the connection between Brother Phillip and Joseph Armwell.

Their final stroke of planning was to have "Brother Phillip" die in the fire. So Joseph Armwell made it look like he was dashing back inside to rescue people, but in the smoke and confusion he easily disappeared. It eliminated all suspicion. After all, an arsonist doesn't die in the fire he started, not if he's trying to collect insurance money.

It would have worked perfectly. Except the real Brother Phillip made a phone call to me in Jamesville.

Why not a plea for help to anyone closer by? Brother Phillip had given it a lot of thought. No one in the street mission neighborhood would believe he was in trouble. After all, they saw him every day. No, Brother Phillip needed someone who had no way of seeing the fake Brother Phillip.

Joseph Armwell bragged time after time what he intended to do. So Brother Phillip pretended to be sicker and sicker every day, while secretly working on his ropes. With Benito's guards around all the time, he doubted he'd be able to escape completely. So one night, the night after the fire, as it happened, he waited until the guard stepped outside for a cigarette, and he broke loose and called Jamesville. Not much of a hope, but his only one.

The guard came back too early. Brother Phillip only had time to remind me of the subway and give me the hint about the end of the circle.

When we showed up, Joseph Armwell knew there would be a search for the real Brother Phillip. He had to come "back to life" to get us to stop searching. So he showed up at the hotel suite and gave us the explanation about a Gulf War flashback.

It worked, of course, but Joseph Armwell didn't know we'd be so determined to get rid of the fake blackmail troubles he and Benito had carefully made in the two months before our arrival.

As we dug into Brother Phillip's past, Joseph and Benito agreed on one final plan, the sting operation involving TV Eleven, especially because of Brother Phillip's connection to Jennifer Mitchell. Along with the chance at more money, each had their reasons for deciding it was the perfect solution. Benito decided it would destroy the exposé series. Joseph wanted to kidnap Joel.

And that's what we knew when the phone call interrupted the discussion.

Jennifer left the table to answer. When she returned, she said, "That's the hospital. Joseph Armwell is out of the coma."

She examined Brother Phillip's face carefully as she told the rest. "He's terrified, Phillip. He nearly died, and he's terrified about the wrong he's done." She paused. "He wants you to visit as soon as possible. He wants to be forgiven. The nurses say he is almost delirious with fear."

Epilogue

Brother Phillip sat completely still for many moments. In the tension, I set down Joel's teddy bear.

Finally Brother Phillip spoke. The tone of each word reminded me of the Brother Phillip who had once been so gentle with words of comfort to me.

He said, "Tell the nurses yes." He thought a moment longer. "Ask them to tell Joseph that God, the One who gives peace, is the One who will forgive him if his heart has truly changed."

Jennifer hurried back to the telephone. There was some silence, then Brother Phillip shrugged shyly. "How can I not forgive him? I've got everything back, don't I?"

Jennifer returned as he was posing the question. She stopped to place second helpings of cheesecake in front of Mike, Ralphy, and me. She moved to behind Brother Phillip at the end of the table, placed her hands on his shoulders, and kissed the top of his head.

"Yes, you dear man. You've got everything back. Including me. Whether you want me or not."

Mike and Ralphy giggled.

"Hold on," I protested. "This whole story you told us about being kidnapped can't be finished yet. What was the reason for Joseph putting you in the guest cottage? Why did he want to kidnap Joel?"

Brother Phillip reached up with crossed arms and held Jennifer's hands on his shoulders. "Because of the end of the circle."

I nodded impatiently. "That's how I guessed where you were. The place of your final good-bye to Jennifer. Where she threw your engagement ring in the pond. Although I went crazy wondering about the pizza order."

Brother Phillip roared with laughter. "Two reasons for that. The guard had caught me on the phone. I faked that I was crazy with delirium and had called a pizza place. That way they wouldn't know I'd gotten through. And the second reason was something real dumb. I kept saying anchovy *fish*, hoping the emphasis on fish would be another clue to the pond."

"Brother Phillip?" Mike said between mouthfuls of cheesecake.

"Yes, Mike?"

"You're right," Mike said. "That was a dumb clue."

"Come on," I said. "Joseph's secret."

"It was the reason he kept me alive," Brother Phillip said. "He thought I knew where the stamps were. Fire insurance money with Benito was a nice bonus, but if he could finally get his hands on the stamps, he'd have it all. Naturally, I couldn't tell him, because I didn't know. But he refused to believe me. In the end, he became so desperate he decided to kidnap Joel and use him as leverage. I tell him, or he'd torture Joel."

Ralphy, who had listened with wide eyes all evening, finally asked a question of his own.

"Who followed us? I mean, there was the taxi that tailed us all the way to the DuBerg mansion. Then someone followed us to Jennifer's apartment."

I barely heard Ralphy. My mind was busy working on another hunch.

I barely heard Dad's reply. "Me, Ralphy. I couldn't let you guys wander around this city without keeping an eye on you."

There was silence, the type of silence you notice in school when a teacher catches you in the middle of a daydream and asks you a question.

I looked up.

Dad repeated his question. "No yells of outrage, Ricky?"

"Huh? No."

My mind snapped back to its problem. *What keeps bothering me?*

I absently stared at the far corner, where Joel was sitting cross-legged and busy with some paper.

"Brother Phillip?" I asked. "Did Joseph say anything at all about those stamps? I mean, why didn't he just keep them when he ran out of the house that afternoon?"

"The answer to that I know very well," Brother Phillip said. "Time and again he told me in the guest cottage how much he hated himself for panicking. Time and again he yelled that he should have just tucked them in his shirt instead of hiding them in my room. But his guilty conscience told him he might be searched if Henry, my father, noticed the stamps were missing before he could flee."

Mr. DuBerg coughed to get our attention. "Funny you should say that. A month later someone posed as a repairman and broke into your room. Nothing was missing. But all the books had been disturbed."

Books!

"Jennifer," I said with heat. "Didn't you tell me you had arrived that afternoon to borrow some textbooks from Phillip?"

She nodded quickly. "But I was so upset that I kept them in the trunk of my car for months. I never opened them once. You don't think that . . ."

She and I both snapped our heads to look for the textbooks she had kept for ten years out of sentimental value.

Gone!

"Joel!" I shouted.

I pushed my chair back and scrambled for traction.

"Joooeeel! Don't lick those stammmps!"

I dove headfirst toward him and managed to lock my hand around his wrist before his tongue could touch the paper he had been playing with.

I collapsed with relief, then held up a sheet of several stamps under a thin wrap of plastic. "Here you are, Mr. DuBerg. Two million dollars' worth of stamps."

He hurried over and examined them, then shouted with glee.

Joel huffed off, grumpy that he couldn't even play mailman without being bothered by grown-ups.

It took several moments for the noise and confusion to die down. And in that confusion I decided to do one final thing, something I had planned ever since receiving the invitation for a celebration supper earlier in the afternoon.

I snuck a small bottle loose from my front pocket and dumped Tabasco sauce into Mike's orange juice.

Two million in stamps or not, a guy's got to have his priorities.